for Bonnelle
&
once again, for Talisa

SHOT IN THE DARK

SHOT IN THE DARK

Janet M. Whyte

James Lorimer & Company Ltd., Publishers
Toronto

James Lorimer & Company Ltd., Publishers acknowledges the support of the Ontario Arts Council. We acknowledge the financial support of the Government of Canada through the Canada Book Fund for our publishing activities. We acknowledge the support of the Canada Council for the Arts, which last year invested $24.3 million in writing and publishing throughout Canada. We acknowledge the Government of Ontario through the Ontario Media Development Corporation's Ontario Book Initiative.

Cover image credit: David Poultney for GOC

Library and Archives Canada Cataloguing in Publication

Whyte, Janet M., author
        Shot in the dark / Janet Whyte.

Issued in print and electronic formats.
ISBN 978-1-4594-0851-7 (bound).--ISBN 978-1-4594-0850-0 (pbk.).--
ISBN 978-1-4594-0852-4 (epub)

        I. Title.

PS8645.H97S56 2015   jC813'.6   C2014-907507-3
C2014-907508-1

James Lorimer & Company Ltd.,
Publishers
317 Adelaide Street West, Suite 1002
Toronto, ON, Canada
M5V 1P9
www.lorimer.ca

Distributed in the United States by:
Orca Book Publishers
P.O. Box 468
Custer, WA, USA
98240-0468

Printed and bound in Canada
Manufactured by Marquis in Montmagny, Quebec in February 2015.
Job #111641

CONTENTS

1 BAD EYE DAY

Here's what I remember.

It was a normal day, more or less. I woke up looking at the world through two snow globes. This freaked me out somewhat. By the time I was ready for school, though, it had settled to pretty much a gentle winter scene. I knew I should tell Mom and Dad. But I really hoped it would get better by itself.

Completely unrealistic thought.

I just didn't want to bother them, you know? They both worked weird hours. Mom was in Customer Service at the Art Gallery — basically selling tickets and telling people how to find the washrooms. Even though that wasn't exactly the plan when she got her Art History degree. But she did get to help hang an exhibit once. She held an Andy Warhol painting of Mickey Mouse that was covered in actual diamond dust! Dad had his own business fixing people's plumbing emergencies. Believe me, you don't want to know the details of that.

Plus, that night's practice was way important. It wasn't a good day to drop everything and zoom over to the Eye Clinic at Vancouver General Hospital. Truth is, I just didn't feel like it.

My parents were both rushing around the kitchen — probably throwing ham onto bread, maybe with a little sauerkraut on Dad's to Ukrainian it up — when I wandered in. "What time do you have to be there?" Mom was asking. "Can you drive Micah to school?"

"I can take the bus," I said, feeling carefully for open cupboard doors as I found cereal and bowl, then spoon and milk. "It's no problem."

"Micah, hi! Good morning," Mom called.

Dad ruffled my hair, which I really hate. It makes me feel like I'm living in a '70s sitcom gone wrong.

"Sure, I can take him," Dad said. "How soon can you be ready, buddy?"

I chewed and swallowed very slowly. *Did I not just suggest I'd take the bus?* I wondered. *Did I maybe only think it, and not say it out loud?* The worst thing about being blind, sometimes, is that you feel invisible, too.

"Hello!?" I shot back. "I must first enjoy my Breakfast of Champions."

"Okay, okay," Dad chuckled. "Ten minutes of breakfast enjoyment, then we're out the door."

"Here's lunch, hon." Mom gave me that quick shoulder squeeze that stands in for a hug now that I'm in high school. "Y'all have a fabulous day now, boys," she drawled as she sailed out. Mom liked to put on this exaggerated Southern accent sometimes, 'cuz she's Black. Like she was swaying down a street in New Orleans listening to old time jazz. But, since she's from Toronto, it didn't actually make sense.

Of course by then Dad was running late. (It's the story of all our lives.) And in our rush to get out the door, I forgot my cane.

Okay, that's not true.

I left it because do you know how much I hate walking with a white cane? Really, really a lot is the answer. It makes me feel like some waif out of a Charles Dickens story. It's bad enough that there are only six Black people in Kitsilano. Okay, I made up that statistic. But you get what I'm saying: I'm already different. The last thing I want is to stagger around with a blind cane. And I *know* everybody is staring at me. And they're all wondering, like: How is he not bumping into that? And I don't actually need a cane because I see fairly well most days. And, for the thing I love most in the world, I don't need to see at all.

What's the thing I love? I'll give you a hint. Not school.

High school was — to quote my favourite comic, Jeremy Hotz — "a festival of awkward moments." For one thing, Kitsilano Secondary had more than 2,000 students. My year alone had more kids than my whole elementary school combined. And, of course, you had to change rooms after every class.

You think parkouring down your crowded school hallway is hard? Try doing it blind! You have to sway past clusters of girls who cannot be separated for a nanosecond. Avoid speed-walking hipsters glued to their phones. Then there are slackers sitting in front of their lockers with their legs out. And don't even get me started on couples joined at the hip. Or jocks running around, fake-shooting hoops wherever they go.

It's a minefield, I'm telling you.

Before Christmas, I'd taken Math (which I'm actually good at), Social Studies (argh), Health (embarrassing), and Physical Education (total "festival of awkward moments"). Now I was taking English (mostly okay), Science (forget about it), Technology (not terrible), and — wait for it —Visual Arts.

I'd signed up as a joke but it turned out that Ms. Zeller was way nice. She tried so hard to encourage me that I was actually doing well! She'd gotten these huge canvasses for me. I was busy covering them with purple and blue blurs that were supposed to be flowers. It was a tribute to Monet, who had also been visually impaired.

In Art, I could be myself. I mean, you can't exactly do it wrong. Who's going to tell you you're making the wrong kind of blurs? Nobody.

Also, in Art, you were allowed to talk. In fact, you were *encouraged* to talk to each other. So that was practically the only class where I knew anyone. I had a place along the wall because, with my eyes, windows kill. Two girls (BFFs) also kept their easels there.

Anna was tall, with blonde hair. I could always pick her out right away. She said everything in this sarcastic tone so I was never sure if she was joking or being serious. Therefore, I was never sure how to respond. When she said she liked my style, was she making fun of me, or what?

The other one, Estelle, was mega-cute. (I mean: What do I know? But, to me, with that dark, curly hair, she was, like, amazing.) She was super encouraging. Sometimes I would ask her about my composition (tone values, spacing of elements, balance, and stuff). She'd always make suggestions. It was the highlight of my day (no pun intended). Even if I didn't 100 per cent follow what she was talking about.

As I was laying out my paintbrushes, I must have been unsteady or something. One of the BFFs noticed.

"Hey, Micah, are you okay?" Anna asked.

"Sure. Well, no," I answered. "I feel kinda rough but don't say anything."

"Okay, I won't post it on Facebook," Anna whispered conspiratorially, "although I do track your every move."

"What?"

"Not!" Anna bumped my shoulder with her shoulder.

"Seriously, what's going on?" Estelle asked.

"I'm having a bad eye day."

"I hate it when that happens!" Anna exclaimed. "You wake up with your eyes all googly, and no amount of mousse or gel will tame them. There's nothing worse!"

Okay, that one made me laugh.

"I just need to get through to this evening," I explained, "because we're having team tryouts right now and I don't want to miss practice."

"Practice for what?" Anna asked.

"Goalball!" I replied, like it was the most obvious thing in the world.

"Sorry," Anna said, "but I'm not totally hip to sports. What's goalball?"

"It's okay. Not a lot of people have heard of it." I paused, trying to figure out a way to describe it. "It's a blind sport — a team sport that you play with a goalball, which is like a bumpy, blue volleyball with bells in it."

"Like a big cat toy?" Estelle asked.

That was only slightly offensive. I took a deep breath and kept going. "Each team has three players on the floor: a Centre and two Wingers. You have to sort of bowl the goalball across the floor of the gym — court, whatever — really fast. So fast the other team can't block it."

"You mean kick it back or what?" Anna asked.

"No, you never kick it," I said, shocked. "You actually play most of the game on the floor, blocking. Then you have to jump up and either pass or throw. Your team only has ten seconds to get the ball back to the other team's side, so it's pretty strenuous. I mean, you're using muscles you didn't even know you had."

There was a pause.

"That came out wrong," I said, snapping my fingers. I'm fairly sure I was blushing.

Anna laughed. "So does it hurt when you block? I mean, when the ball hits you?"

"It hurts when the ball *doesn't* hit you," I answered. "Because if it gets past you, and into your net, the other team scores."

"So is a goalball net like a soccer net?" Anna asked.

"Kind of," I said. "But not so high, and it's wider."

"I begin to understand," Anna said in a fake-serious voice.

"And what are we painting today?" Ms. Zeller asked teasingly, checking our canvasses.

"I'm trying cubism," Estelle jumped in, showing Ms. Zeller the progress of her work. It was lucky Estelle was such a keener because I didn't even have my paints ready. I bustled around, trying to look busier than I actually was.

After Ms. Zeller moved on, I whispered: "One last thing: Everybody has to wear blackout eyeshades."

"What are blackout eyeshades? I want some!" Anna stage-whispered back.

"They're like a mask every player has to wear so we'll all have the same level of vision."

"What do you mean? What level of vision?" Estelle asked.

"None at all," I answered. "When you play goalball, you're completely, totally blind."

2 FLARE-UP

By now you've guessed the thing I love. Goalball. That's my sport. Sometimes I feel like everything else is just filler and I'm only alive once I hit the court. Blood starts rushing past my ears as soon as I put on my gear: hockey shorts; what our coach, Stephan, calls "protection for Area 51"; knee pads; elbow pads; runners.

I slung my eyeshades over one wrist and began warm-up. I started running a familiar track around the outer edge of the Collins Community Centre gym. I could hear tape ripping. Lauren's parents were setting up the goalball court by taping thin ropes to the floor.

Brad, a Paralympic athlete and one of my heroes, fell into step. "Hey, Micah," he drawled.

"I'll never figure out how you know it's me before I even say anything!"

"It's not hard, with that weird Igor limp you've got."

"What? I don't . . ."

"And you're always the first one out here." He laughed. "So I feel I can hazard a guess."

"Oh," I said, 'cuz I'm just that good at snappy comebacks.

"Brad, Micah, will you guys do me a favour?" Coach called. He was balancing the ball Globetrotters-style as we jogged over. The internal bells jangled like even the goalball couldn't wait to get started.

"If you would each check a Team Area for me, we'll be good to go."

"I'll take this side," Brad said, his voice receding.

I jogged the other way, past runners and people doing floor exercises. I knelt down and ran one hand all around the rectangle that marked the Team Area. The lines were straight. The rope was obvious enough that we could find it by touch during a game. The tape that stuck down the rope was smooth so no one would trip.

I checked our side's net, which ran straight across and covered the back wall of our Team Area. Then I checked the wing lines that were halfway between the Team Area's front line and the goal net. One for the Left Winger, and one for the Right Winger. Finally, I found the small middle line — smack in the centre of the Team Area. Just a tiny piece of rope at a right angle to the front line. It may seem crazy, but when you're running around blind, you need fast ways to figure out where you are. "It's perfect, Coach," I yelled.

"Thanks, Micah. Okay, everybody! Lauren and Marcus, you'll be on Brad's team. Amir, Brandon, and

Jorge will be substitutes. Sebastian and Alyssa are on Micah's side."

I put on my eyeshades and the darkness was complete. This always shocked me, at first, because I normally saw quite a lot. Even if, some days, it was like living inside a snowscape of light and shadow. Now, there was nothing at all.

The whistle blew. "The coin toss goes to" — Coach paused — "Brad."

"We'll stay on this end and throw first," Brad decided.

Big surprise. Under the eyeshade, I was rolling my eyes.

"Okay, let's do a few court warm-ups," Coach called. I oriented myself to the middle of the Team Area. I heard Coach throw the ball and followed the sound as it bounced toward me. I caught it, jumped to throwing position, and hurled it back. Then I ran out of the Team Area as the next player zipped into position. We did this until the whistle blew again.

"Five minutes," our referee, Julie, announced. Julie was the assistant coach, but she doubled during practices as ref. She walked over and checked all our eyeshades, per International Blind Sports Federation rules. We tried to play by the regulations as much as possible. But in a real tournament, each team would have six players — three on the floor and three alternates. Also, even though we practised together, actual teams are never coed.

"Sebastian, you're Right Wing," I said. "Alyssa, you'll be Centre." At the thirty second whistle, I found the left wing line. I knew I was in position. I crouched, balanced on my left foot with my right leg out to the side. Totally ready to throw myself across my part of the Team Area and stop the ball. Anything to protect our net.

"Quiet, please," Julie said. Then: "Play!"

When the ball comes all the way across the gym, it rings fairly loud. I slid across the floor into blocking position as the goalball bounced toward our team. It skimmed down the right side of the court and jingled as Sebastian stopped it. I heard a scuffle as he jumped up to throw.

Alyssa knocked on the floor to show us where she was. It was a way to tell us she was kneeling, compacting herself into a sort-of fetal position. Basically, it was so she wouldn't get hit in the back of the head. Pushing off with both hands, I jumped to a crouch and moved to the back corner of my Team Area, clapping so Sebastian would know my position and could pass to me. But, instead he ran forward, did a spin to gain speed, then threw the goalball super hard to the other net.

Clang! The ball bounced once and hit someone, probably Marcus. Oh, yeah. Definitely Marcus. I heard him exclaim as the ball whipped over him, whooshing into the net.

"Point!" Julie called. "Play!"

Marcus whammed the ball back at us. He must have been mad because it crashed sideways down the court, right to Sebastian. Before anybody could move, Sebastian had whipped it back across the gym again.

No doubt about it, the guy could throw! And it was a good thing he was fast because we only had seconds to get the ball across the court's centre line. But was he planning to play the whole game by himself? *Come on, man,* I thought, *stop being such a show-off! Give somebody else a chance!*

I could tell that the ball had hit Marcus again. This time, he was ready. He caught it and passed, I guessed, to Brad.

And now, I thought, *the game begins.*

I should probably admit that I have the bad habit of visualizing everything in my mind. Even though that's kind of a time waster. Sort of like translating words back into English when you're trying to speak French, instead of just speaking French. So if I sound like I actually saw the game happening, well, that's because I did.

Brad threw the ball gently, with a tinkling bounce and an almost-soundless roll.

What I called a Silent Killer.

I flopped across my end of our Team Area, listening hard, trying to picture the ball. *Where was it?*

A jangle as Alyssa grabbed it, then:

"Here!"

Alyssa threw the ball toward Sebastian's urgent voice. She crouched, knocking to show that she was down on the floor, out of the way.

"Hey! No!" I shouted, in a voice full of edgy frustration. But it was too late.

Sebastian had hurled the ball again.

How can I describe what came next? You know the old saying, "seeing red"? That's actually what happened. It just flooded my mind and I found myself yelling in this mean, exasperated way, "Learn to count, you guys!"

You don't throw more than twice in a row! I ranted to myself. *And you totally know that, Sebastian!* I felt my face getting way hot. *What a ball hog! Just stupid and . . .*

"Useless!" I screamed out loud. "You're useless!" Then I did something terrible.

I threw my eyeshades and stormed off the court.

3 IDIOPATHIC

Then I was in the locker room and I didn't know what to do next. I felt ridiculous. So there was that, I guess. Check. Mission accomplished.

Why did I do that? I agonized.

More to the point: *Why did I do that in front of practically everyone I know?*

I collapsed onto the bench that took up the whole middle of the room. *Maybe I should just lie here forever?* At that moment, it seemed like a pretty appealing thought.

"So what the *hey* was that?" When he was upset, Coach talked fast and sounded especially French-Canadian.

I threw my arm over my eyes. "Coach, I'm sorry," was all I could choke out.

"I don't know what's going on with you but I want to say that was not acceptable."

"I know."

"*And* you were wrong. I told you last time: The two-throw rule has changed. It no longer applies."

My face was red. Instead of admitting I forgot, though, I mumbled, "Yeah, but you said we should still observe it, even though it's not official."

Weak, I know.

"That's our *strategy,*" Coach snapped. "I don't want one player throwing all the time and getting injured. You guys need to learn to pass."

"Were you planning on telling Sebastian that?" I sneered.

Also weak.

Not to mention: terrible timing.

"I think you should call it a night, Micah." In the doorway, Coach turned. "Just one more thing . . ."

I almost smirked because no adult ever just says one more thing. It's always, like, at least seven more things.

"Practice is for everyone! Everybody gets to participate! You have to be a little bit patient!"

I uncovered my eyes in time to observe the famous "Stephan shrug."

He waved his hands over his head, appealing to the universe. Like, there must be intelligent life *somewhere*! "There are only about thirty goalball players in B.C.," Stephan lectured. "Most of them are here in Vancouver, which is why we have two practice groups. And most of them are in your age range, sure. But we also have National Team players and even guys training for the Paralympics. Mixed in with that are people who just want exercise. Everyone gets to play, but they're not all going to be perfect!"

Coach paused and shook his head. "Look, you have talent, Micah. You're one of my up-and-coming Junior players. Justify my faith in you, okay?"

"I'll try," I nodded. "I mean, I will."

"For somebody who hasn't been playing long, you're good. You're already on the Junior Team, as far as I'm concerned. You just need to complete your orientation test and you're in. So let's keep it together until then, eh?"

"Do you think I'll make it to the Regional Tournament?"

"Sure. And if they have a trophy for Most Unsportsmanlike Conduct, you'll get that, too."

I threw him a sideways look — with what I hoped was a somewhat charming grin. "I honestly am sorry, Coach."

"Don't worry about it," he said, "but I'm not the one you need to apologize to, you know? I'll see you Wednesday."

I sat with my head down for a while. I considered asking Dad to pick me up early. But then I realized I'd need to tell him why.

I decided to wait out front.

It was one of those early spring sunsets that seem way too bright to me. The light made everything shimmer with a neon glow. I slumped onto a bench at the community centre's entrance, the one that was usually taken up by old guys. You know the kind I mean? Whose mission in life is to camp out there criticizing the government? Lucky for me, they'd all gone home.

One reason I don't like to stop moving is that, sometimes, I'll start to think. So of course all the things Coach had said were rattling around in my head. Not the part about poor sportsmanship, which I sort of already knew. The part about how I was good for someone who hadn't been playing goalball very long. It made me feel like an impostor. Like I hadn't earned my stripes or something.

The whole "belonging" thing has always been tricky for me. I've always been a one-foot-in/one-foot-out kind of guy.

I've had eye disease my whole life but only became "officially" visually impaired about a year and a half ago. B3. That's me. Or maybe I should say that's my Paralympic medical classification. My sight is 6/60, which means I see at six metres what most sighted people can see at sixty metres. In other words, ten per cent.

The worst part about having uveitis — besides, you know, going *blind* and all — is that it's just always there, day after day, in everything you do. My life has been one solid round of doctors. Anti-inflammatories. Eye drops. Intravenous corticosteroids. And more doctors. Most of the time, I get iritis, which is inflammation of the coloured part of the eye (in my case, blue). Sometimes I get panuveitis, which is inflammation of the whole thing. When I was a little kid, a doctor explained that my eye disease was "idiopathic." Later, I understood he was saying there was no known cause. But, at the time, I thought he meant I was stupid, too.

I knew I should tell Dad I was having another attack.

That I was *maybe* having another attack.

After my last flare-up, my irises were permanently scarred. You know how old glass gets bumpy and runny? It was like I was stuck in an ancient house, looking out at the world through warped windows.

This just didn't seem as *bad* as last time, though. That time, my eyes went completely red, and they totally hurt. Like, unbearably. I really had no choice but to go to the hospital. But this time, things were just unfocused.

Story of my life, when you think about it.

If I were to graph it, you'd see a Sad Downward Slide, a Panicky Swoop, and then a Resigned Levelling Off. And do you want to know the one good thing that came out of it? The only good thing? Goalball. I finally found something I was good at! Something I could keep doing no matter what.

Want to hear the worst thing about the Sad Downward Slide? Never knowing how bad it was going to get. It's never fun to slowly lose something bit by bit. But some things are easier to fix than others. I mean, you can't exactly get an eye toupee. Or would it be called an eyepiece? Anyway, you know what I'm saying.

One of the awesome things, though, was spending more time with my mom. She wanted me to see all the art she loved while I still could. And it was a lot of art! Impressionists, Neo-Impressionists, Post-Impressionists, Modernists, *Fauves* — and that was just the Europeans! Also there was the Group of Seven, Emily Carr, Paul Morin, Ted Harrison, et cetera and et cetera. Ever since then, whenever I describe my vision as "Monet-ish" or "like a Seurat," Mom and Dad know exactly what I mean.

We also spent lots of time at the R.H. MacMillan Space Centre and Observatory because Dad is a huge astronomy buff and a card-carrying member of the Royal Astronomical Society. As a result, I know every planet in our solar system and every type of galaxy in deep space. Quasars, black holes, nebulae . . . And, as long as I'm facing north, I can show you every constellation in our night sky.

I glanced up and there was Dad, walking toward me through the deep blue twilight. At that moment, I was grateful he'd made me look at so many stars.

4 SKILLS

"Okay, we're going to do Micah's orientation test now," Coach announced, "so take five, everybody, and get some water."

Now? "We can do that after the game, Coach," I suggested oh-so-casually.

"Now is good. Brandon will keep score."

Great! I'm sure a Paralympic athlete will be happy to let all my mistakes slide.

"Micah, start with position A."

I walked to one end of the gym and stood alone on the right side of the Team Area, not feeling singled out or anything. (*Sure!*) I imagined the Team Area divided into five positions going right to left: A through E. I pulled on my eyeshades. "Ready," I said.

The fact that everyone (and by "everyone" I mean the people who'd witnessed my freak-out just forty-eight hours earlier) was sitting on the bench watching me didn't make me nervous at all.

That was a lie. I had to tune them out, though,

because this test was really, really important. It was the only thing standing between me and a spot on the Junior Team.

Coach tossed me a goalball. "One through five," he instructed.

In my mind, I saw the numbered positions as five Iron Man–type laser sightings. in the other Team Area Position one was in the opposite corner: as far left as I could hurl the goalball without throwing out. Two was halfway between the edge of the court and the middle, where the Centre played. Three was dead centre (although you're not actually supposed to kill that player). Four was halfway between the middle and the right side of the court. Five was straight across from me.

"Ready?" Coach asked.

"Yes."

I focused, visualizing the opposite corner of the gym. Rotated my right arm, and threw. I heard the goalball bounce, skitter across the floor. There was a soft *whump* as Brandon caught it.

I let out a slow breath. I'd managed a diagonal shot without throwing out of bounds. Not easy, especially for me.

It was true, what they said about goalball: "It's not hard to learn it, but it's hard to get *good* at it." The truth is, my throwing wasn't very powerful yet. Brandon had the fastest throw in Canada, maybe even the world.

So feebly trickling the ball toward him was kind of embarrassing.

My next shot would be to position two. Coach chucked me another goalball. Stepping back, I leaned down to feel the right wing position line to make sure I was actually facing forward.

I whipped the ball as hard as I could. Heard it smack into the net. *Nuts,* I thought — only that's not what I actually thought. In reality, I used a much harsher word.

Usually you *want* to get the ball into the goal net. In this case, though, it meant I'd missed Brandon. Which meant I'd missed the shot.

"Slow it down, Micah," Coach advised. "We're going for accuracy here."

Oh, is one out of two not accurate?

Focus, Micah! I told myself.

Coach rolled me another ball. I picked it up, oriented myself, and threw to dead centre.

Yes! A ringing thump told me I'd made it.

Now for position four, between the middle spot and the one on the right. My throw seemed to take forever to hit the floor. It trickled across the gym with a slow, spangling roll.

"High ball," Coach said. "In a game, that would be a penalty, Micah."

I nodded vigorously.

Finally, position five: straight ahead to the corner in front of me. (And, being the easiest shot, sort of a specialty of mine.) I took a risk and put on speed, whamming the goalball across the court.

I heard a satisfying, resounding *smack* as Brandon caught the ball. I allowed myself a small smile.

"Good job," Coach said. "Now move to B."

We did the whole thing again from B position, then in C position at centre. With every set, fewer balls missed Brandon. With every throw, I felt more confident.

By D, I was exhausted.

"Do you need a break, Micah? You want some water?" Coach asked.

"No, thank you. I'm good," I puffed.

By the time we got to E position, I was gritting my teeth. My left eye had developed a vicious ache. Did I work best under pressure? Did desperation, in my case, breed excellence? I had no idea.

But I was making almost every shot.

"Very good!" Coach finally said. "Well done, Micah. You want to know your results?"

I collapsed onto my back. "No," I croaked. I was reasonably sure I'd done well but I didn't feel like having everybody else hear. "Just text me, okay?"

"You got it," Coach said. "Now, let's play! Brandon, Alyssa, Marcus, you're one team. Brad, Amir, and Lauren, you're the other. Sebastian and Micah are alternates."

I slid my eyeshades to the top of my head. I was relieved to sit out for a while but nervous about Sebastian. I pretended to be winded so he wouldn't expect me to talk.

Awkward.

Brandon's team won the coin toss. Each side grouped, deciding who would play which position. Julie checked their eyeshades, and they were ready.

"Quiet! Play!" she hollered.

It was like watching a tennis game rocked by six people. Brad, as Centre, seemed to be everywhere. Blocking, bouncing to his feet, throwing. He always aimed at the opposing team's toes, where he was most likely to smooth a goal through.

And Brandon was in full powerhouse mode. His shots were mostly directed at Lauren — and she blocked them nearly every time. Sometimes she threw, but more often, she passed the ball to Brad or Amir.

"Good strategy," I whispered, hoping Sebastian would take the hint.

"Better than throwing equipment?" he asked innocently.

Ouch.

"Let's give Lauren a break," Coach said. "Sebastian, you're in. Micah, substitute for Brandon."

Gratefully, I ran to take Brandon's spot — Left Wing — as I pulled my eyeshades down. I found my position line and crouched behind it, ready to throw myself in the front of the ball.

"Play!" Julie yelled.

The goalball came at me, ringing hard. I blocked it with my shins and scrambled to my feet. "Got it," I told my teammates. I checked the wing line to make sure I was facing forward. Then I ran, and threw.

Sebastian snagged it; fired it back.

This time I extended my arms and caught the goalball neatly with my face. I fumbled. The ball spun away off the tips of my fingers.

I was glad the other players were wearing eyeshades.

"Block out," Julie said, throwing the ball back to me. "Play!"

I was also grateful that, for us butterfingers, goalball was a forgiving sport. Even though the ball went out of bounds, my block counted. The ball was still in my team's control.

I checked my position again and threw, torquing the goalball toward Brad, the other team's Centre player. It came back, almost before I could get into defensive position, and whacked me in the gut. I grabbed the ball with both hands. Managed to get to my knees. Couldn't get up.

"Al," I whispered. "Alyssa, are you there?"

"Here!" she called.

I tossed the ball toward the sound. Now, both of my eyes *killed*.

The action moved to the right side of the court. Even though I kept stretching into block position like a total keener, the ball never came to me again. Which was lucky because I was having trouble figuring out where it was.

Julie blew the whistle, signalling an end to the half, and I pushed up my eyeshades.

"We're low on time, everybody, so that'll be it for today," Coach said. "But you're all doing great. The Regional Tournament is coming up, and you Junior level guys will know in the next few days whether or not you made the team. We've also got the Provincial Championship happening this summer, so our Senior guys will need to stay focused on that. Good job, everybody! Micah, you did well tonight."

"Way to go," Sebastian whispered.

"Thanks!" *Did that mean I'd made it?*

I hoped it meant I'd made it.

"See you Friday," Coach concluded, unnecessarily.

As we wandered into the locker room, I heard three or four different conversations:

"Thanks, Coach."

"Excellent!"

"Great throwing tonight."

". . . gotta improve our defence . . ."

I didn't participate in any of the talks. Just sunk into the background and slid out of there.

5 VANCOUVER GENERAL HOSPITAL

This is how it happened.

The next morning my vision was worse. Way worse. Like, *Parents Freaking Out and Medical Personnel Yelling* worse. I decided to go to the Vancouver General Hospital Eye Clinic. Casually drop in before school, like you do.

I stomped out with this *so in a hurry* attitude and headed for the door.

"Hi, hon! How did things go yesterday?" Mom called. "Do you have your results yet?"

"My results?"

"From your orientation test!"

"Oh. No. I don't know yet. I feel good about it, though."

"Well, great. Are you having breakfast?"

"No, I've got to meet my . . . study group," I lied, "before school. We're meeting in the library." I was terrible at deception.

"What sort of study group?" she asked mildly.

I heard a page turn, probably a page of the morning paper. I figured she wasn't actually paying attention.

"Earth Science. We're studying sedimentary layers, metamorphic rock. Schist like that."

She laughed out loud, so I guess she was listening. "I don't work until later, so if you can wait ten minutes, I'll give you a lift," she offered.

"I'll take the bus!" I said irritably. "And I can buy lunch today. Don't worry so much!"

"Are you sure?" She sounded dubious.

"I'm sure," I called. "See you tonight."

Whew. I unfolded my cane — definitely necessary today due to whiteout conditions — and tapped the edge of the top stair. Three steps down. Six more steps to the cast-iron gate that protected our microscopic front yard. Through the gate. Turn left on the sidewalk. *Yeah, you've got this.*

Living in Kitsilano was like living in a small town. A very *expensive* small town.

Walk three short blocks. Check. Press the crossing signal. No problem. Wait for the chirping sound to show it's my turn to go. Okay. And step off the curb.

Of the things that came next — cane skittering away, weird pressure down my side — I remember the sounds of screaming the most. I had never heard sounds like that, ever. They were like movie screams! As helpful as the shrieking was, I was more grateful when someone finally looked under the front of the car and said,

"Are you okay?"

I had curled into a fetal position. "Not sure?" I answered.

"I called 9-1-1," a man said. "An ambulance will be here soon."

"Thank you." I scooched forward, goalball-style.

"Uh, I don't think you should move."

"I'm good," I said, and climbed out. "Has anybody seen my cane?"

"I hit a *blind* kid?" a woman's voice sobbed theatrically.

Yes, let's all feel sorry for you. I thought. *You hit a blind kid.*

I bent my knees and bounced slightly. "Seems alright," I said.

A girl handed me my cane. "Come sit here. It's safer."

"Thanks." I perched on the edge of a planter. "Thank you, everybody."

I'd been hit by a red Jeep — actually a very nice truck. The driver was all agitated, explaining to everyone that she had been turning right. Which was obvious.

"I'm really okay," I said, reassuringly. "This is a lot of hassle over nothing." But the hassle had just begun.

The fire department arrived. Then the police got there and, with stern words, took the crying lady aside. I actually felt sorry for old Right Turn, even if it was all her fault.

A paramedic knelt beside me and asked what had happened. That same second, he whipped out a flashlight and shone it — *blam* — into my eye.

It was *excruciating*. "Gahhh!" I squawked, flinching away. "Quit that!!"

"I'm trying to see if you have a concussion."

"I don't," I said, "but I *do* have uveitis. I was on my way to Vancouver General."

"By yourself?"

"I'll call my mom," I sighed.

"Don't worry about that now. They'll call her from the hospital." *So much for Mom's relaxing morning.* "What's your name?"

I wanted to say *Bond. James Bond. B*ut instead I whispered meekly: "Micah Janzen."

"Does anything hurt?"

"Just my eyes," I said. To my shock, a tear slid down my face.

Because of the eye disease, I swear.

They put me on a gurney like I was ninety. To tell you the truth, I was starting to feel about that old. They lifted me into the ambulance.

"Tired?" The ambulance guy smiled. "It's the adrenaline. Once it wears off, you feel like you could sleep for a week. Don't worry. You're going to be fine." Then he called: "Ready for transport. Code 2." Which meant we just drove normally with no siren. Kind of a bummer.

The ambulance paramedic slid on a pressure cuff and pumped it up. Meanwhile, I was replaying everything. *What happened to Ol' Yeller?* I wondered. *Maybe she's in a different ambulance right now, on her way to the psych ward. She'll probably be ahead of me in the emergency room. And they'll probably take care of her first! Because it seems like sighted people always . . .*

"Whoa, your blood pressure just spiked," the paramedic exclaimed. "What's going on?" He listened to my heart.

Since I'd just been run over at an intersection *when it was my turn to walk*, yeah, I was angry!

"Heart rate's up, too," he said.

I tried to reel myself in. "Who was doing all the screaming?" I asked.

"It was the guy who called us, wasn't it?"

I couldn't help it. I laughed. "I'm pretty sure it was a *woman*," I pointed out.

"Whoever they were, I'll bet they were relieved to see you get up. Not everyone does."

Before I could respond to that happy thought, we were at the hospital. The paramedics unloaded the gurney and wheeled me into the ER.

A doctor fell into step beside us. "What have we got?" she asked.

"Ped strike," the ambulance guy said. "He's a minor: Micah Janzen. No visible lacerations or broken bones, but he may be concussed. He's got something wrong with his eyes." They wheeled me into a curtained slot.

"Thanks, guys," the doctor called. "We'll take it from here."

"Yeah, thank you," I told their retreating backs.

"So Micah," the doctor said. "The first thing we'd better do is call your parents."

I reluctantly recited our home number.

"Thanks. Get into this gown and I'll be back."

I changed super quickly because you never know who's going to come barging in. Sure enough, the doctor ducked past the curtain seconds later. "Your mother will be here soon. I'm Dr. Lu, by the way."

"It's nice to meet you," I said.

"Nice to meet you. Your mom tells me you're a regular at our Eye Clinic here, so I've asked an eye specialist to come over. Do you know Dr. Blocker?"

"Yeah," I nodded. "I've seen him lots."

"That's fine. Now where were you hit? Can you raise your arm? Let me see your hip . . ." And et cetera until I was completely checked out.

Not embarrassing at all.

"Knock knock." Dr. Blocker walked in, focused on my chart. "So, Micah, what's happening?"

"I'm having a flare-up. I know I should have said something . . . Sorry."

"Looks painful. When did it begin?"

"Um, yesterday?" I said uncertainly, "something like that?"

"Something like that," he said doubtfully and turned to Dr. Lu. "Please have Micah transferred to the Eye Care Centre, bed three. I'll need to examine him right away."

"Absolutely," Dr. Lu said, and ducked out.

"See you over there," Dr. Blocker concluded. I pictured him giving me his usual raised-eyebrows kind of smile.

Then this strange guy came — an orderly, I guess? He took me down a long hallway to a weird old abandoned tunnel. It was probably from the 1800s. You know, with oozing walls and creepy old wheelchairs and stuff?

Nah, I'm just messing with you. It was just an ordinary hall. Still, I was dreading what I knew would be next.

The worst part wasn't the yellow freezing stuff Dr. Blocker squeezed into each eye. Or bright lights blazing into my skull as he examined them. It wasn't the part where he said: "You know better than this, Micah! I told you last time, if you suspect you're having a flare — if you even *think* the word flare — you have to come in right away. You can't wait even a day!"

It wasn't even when he told my mom that I had to stay in the hospital overnight for "aggressive treatment." Or when he reminded her that I had cataracts and was legally blind.

And although it was awful hearing my mom's worried, disappointed voice saying, "Oh, Micah, oh, no," that still wasn't the most horrible thing. The worst part was when she told Dad . . .

I'm not 100 per cent sure, because by then my eyes were full of medicine and I couldn't see anything. But I'm fairly sure . . .

He cried.

6 PUSH

So I'll tell you how it felt: a freezing cold drip, dripping into my arm. The chill circulated everywhere before settling in my head. It tasted gunmetal gray. I hated it.

Even though I was totally wiped, I couldn't sleep, so I just lay there forever. I couldn't even stare at the ceiling because everything had this strange glow. It was hot in there, too, I guess because the hospital was full of people with poor circulation.

I felt terrible, is what I'm trying to say.

If I fell asleep for a nanosecond, a nurse would show up to check my I.V. or cram drops into my eyes. The whole night was basically freeze-dried, metal-tasting, unfocused discomfort. Then it was time to choke down scrambled eggs and non-crispy wheat toast accompanied by a teeny plastic cup of apple juice.

Joy.

I know that Dad drifted in at one point, but I guess by then I was demented with fatigue or something. I could barely wake up enough to say two words. But by the time I'd had my tasty breakfast, I only needed eye drops every four hours instead of every two. Four hours seemed like a huge amount of sleep to get all at once!

So, by lunchtime, I was actually feeling pretty good. And life got way better once a nurse came to take out my I.V.

I heard my mom and dad talking in the hallway, discussing me with a doctor, I guess. Then Dad came in with a big bunch of *Get Well* helium mylars.

"Hey, how many balloons am I holding up?"

"Funny," I said.

Mom sat on the edge of the bed and pushed the hair out of my eyes, like moms do. "How are you feeling?"

"Good. A lot better!"

Mom glanced at Dad. Dad pulled a chair close and sat down. I felt surrounded. A serious talk was on the horizon.

"Micah," Dad said. "You know you can't delay treatment when you have eye disease. Why didn't you say anything?"

How could I tell them that I was tired of everything being *all about me all the time*? I mean, it's fine to be your parents' whole world when you're eight, but once you hit thirteen, you kind of want them to get a life of their own.

"You were busy," I mumbled. *Super weak.*

"We're never too busy for you!" Mom exclaimed. "It's just that we thought if something was going on, you would tell us." She sounded sad.

It dawned on me that they *had* been trying to let me be more independent. And that I'd blown it. "I'm really sorry," I mumbled.

"Look," Dad said. "I checked the waiting list and . . ."

I'm going to jump in here and explain that by "waiting list," he meant the waiting list for a guide dog. It was complicated. Even though I kept saying I wasn't sure, they had more or less nagged me into applying for one last summer.

It wasn't that I didn't want a dog. I'd always wanted a dog! But did I want a dog with me all the time, everywhere I went?

Did I want every eye on me when we got on the bus?

And then, when the driver announced an available "courtesy seat" and described where it was, even people who were reading their newspapers or whatever would stop and stare as I sat down and made the dog curl up by my feet. Everybody would watch me and no one would say a word.

That's exactly what would happen. I knew, because it's what I did.

But then I was on the waiting list at B.C. and Alberta Guide Dog Services, so it was all a done deal.

". . . so they explained that now you'll need to get serious about your orientation and mobility training." Dad had been talking this whole time.

And I kept nodding even though I'd probably missed a few things.

"We mean it, Micah," he concluded. "You can't wuss out after a few sessions like you did last time. You need to actually complete the program."

"Okay."

"The CNIB is sending someone over next week," Mom chimed in. "His name is Cam Johnson and he's visually impaired himself."

"Orientation and Mobility Specialists are usually sighted," Dad announced proudly, like it was something he'd just learned. "But they said that Cam is extremely good at navigation."

Night navigation, I thought, even though that didn't actually make sense as a metaphor. The Milky Way blazed across my mind and I imagined myself alone, in some kind of desert, under a million stars I could no longer see.

"Anyway, you'll likely be released from the hospital this afternoon, so we can talk about this more at home," Mom said.

"Excuse me," a nurse interrupted, "but we need to take Micah for his eye exam now." An orderly helped me into a wheelchair — which was unnecessary but kind of fun — and took me took me to the examination room. Then, after the whole eye-freezing, light-blazing routine, Dr. Blocker told me that my eyes were better. "It doesn't look like this flare-up caused further damage," he said, "so you're lucky."

Sure, I thought, *I'm very, very lucky.*

Then I wondered: *Exactly how much school will I be able to skip without missing any goalball?*

Dad drove us home from the hospital. Mom sat in the front passenger seat but kept twisting around, looking at me. Like maybe she was afraid I might disintegrate.

"How are you feeling, really?" she asked, sounding concerned.

"I'm good," I said. "My eyes still feel weird — like maybe they need more rest — but I'm okay."

"Maybe Micah shouldn't go back to school right away, Richard," Mom said. "Maybe he should stay home a least a few days next week. He has to rest his eyes. Then he can get started on his orientation and mobility training and he won't be too tired."

"Yeah," Dad agreed. "Since you're on afternoons, I'll make sure I'm home early. It shouldn't be a problem."

"I can probably manage *not* to burn the house down if I'm home alone for a few hours," I joked.

"Hmm," Mom said dubiously. "I guess you'd have to work at it to start a fire in a microwave."

I laughed. "I'll keep the extinguisher handy. But, seriously, I feel fine! I think I can even make practice tonight." I tried to look energetic. Not an easy task considering how much medication was still running through my veins.

"You're seriously up to that?" Mom sounded worried.

"I'm okay! The doctor said so!"

"I'm not sure it's a good idea." Mom was shaking her head — always a bad sign.

"I'll take him," Dad jumped in. "Maybe just stick to warm-up exercises for a while, eh, buddy, and sit out the games? Anyway, I'll tell Coach that you need to go easy."

"Okay, Richard. But if you and Stephan break my kid, you know what will happen!"

"Heads! Will! Roll!" Dad and I yelled, grinning.

We finished dinner late, so I ended up being one of the last players to arrive at the community centre. I guess news travels, though, because every single guy in the locker room asked how I was doing. It was kind of dazzling. Finally, I got out to the court, ready to warm up.

And then I heard a voice I'd never encountered before. It said: "Who am I looking at?"

I held out my hand. "I'm Micah. Who am I introducing myself to?"

"Liam," he said with a bone-crushing handshake. "I just moved here from the Valley."

"Liam's been on the Valley's Junior Team for the past two years," Sebastian piped up.

"Glad to meet you, Liam," I lied, but really I was thinking: *Crap! You turn your back for a second and suddenly some guy's here — some athlete guy who's been on the Junior Team for years — and then it's all about him!*

I remembered Liam. Or maybe I should say, I remembered hearing everybody rave about Liam after last year's Regional Tournament. They all kept going on and on about how much Liam had deserved to be MVP. How he had this mega-fast, super accurate throw. How his blocking was off-the-charts awesome. In general — how totally perfect he was.

Then I thought: *We'll just see about that.*

7 ORIENTATION

I was way happy to stay home, lying on the couch, watching TV. I guess I *was* still tired from the hospital because I was asleep when Cam arrived. And possibly even drooling.

"Hi, Micah? I'm Cam from the CNIB."

"Hi, yep." I flailed a bit, trying to sit up. "Hello."

"Your mom let me in. Sorry if I caught you at a bad time."

"No, no, it's good. I'm good," I mumbled. I shook his hand in this limp-fish sort of way. I'm sure I made a terrific first impression.

"Is it okay if I sit with you awhile?" Cam asked.

"Sure," I said, "there's a chair on your right."

Cam folded his cane in one smooth motion, stepped in front of the chair, and sat down. He didn't even check to make sure it was there! He just believed me.

And I felt a bit humbled by that.

"Do you feel up to talking? Or do you want me to start?"

"You go."

"Hi, I'm Cam," he said, parodying the whole AA introduction they always show in movies. "And I'm a non-visual learner . . ."

I had to think about that for a second.

". . . I work for the CNIB part-time as a mild-mannered Orientation and Mobility Specialist, but I also have a secret identity."

"Really."

"Yes, as a master's degree student at UBC."

"In what?"

"Educational and Counselling Psychology, and Special Education. In other words, I'm studying to be a school counsellor. But, if I'm truly lucky, I'll get to design educational experiences."

I squinted a little. "What?"

"I want to help kids learn in different ways. To help them have direct experiences instead of just reading about things or being told things."

"Uh-huh."

"Anyway. Enough about me. Your turn."

"Okay. I go to Kits — I mean, Kitsilano Secondary. I'm in Grade 8. I'm a fantastic student — probably gonna be on the honour roll this year. I major in biology. And I'm on the football team."

"Wow!"

"That's . . . um . . . actually, I stink at school. Especially science. Even when my eyes were good, I couldn't see anything through a microscope. I've never ever seen anything through a microscope! And now I can't even read the blackboard unless I put on super-thick nerd glasses and walk right up to it."

"Still, it's fantastic you made the football team!" Cam said.

I burst out laughing. When it came to sarcasm, I'd met my match. "Ah . . . no," I said, "but I do play goalball."

"Really? Or are you imagining things again? 'Cuz we can get a shrink over here right away . . ."

"I'm fine," I said.

"You're sure?" Cam asked. "We're sharing the same reality now?"

"Yes, I'm sure."

"Very good. So can you tell me about your vision? I mean, I know you have uveitis, but can you tell me when you see best and when you have problems?"

"Well, when I'm inside, like, if there's normal indoor lighting, I see okay," I said. "I see big gestures and can usually tell if somebody's smiling or laughing. But when I go outside or if someone turns on a light, it takes my eyes a long time to adjust. Sometimes I can't see anything at all."

"Yeah, I went through that, too," Cam said. "It's frustrating."

"I know, right?" I said. "I have these harsh, vampire-strength sunglasses and even they don't help sometimes."

"Are you a vampire?"

"Pretty much, except for the seeing-in-the-dark part and the human-blood-drinking part."

"I'm getting the picture. So let's practise some orientation skills right now. I know you wouldn't normally use your cane in the house — since you know where everything is — but let's just run through a few techniques."

"Okay," I said. I unfolded my cane, which Mom had just happened to place on the coffee table. "But I already know how to walk with a cane."

"Good. Humour me anyway. Maybe close your eyes to make it more challenging."

I got up with a sigh and an exaggerated eye roll. I slowly walked across our family room using two-point touch, moving my cane left as my right foot came forward, then swinging it to the right as my left foot moved. I hit something and stopped. I tapped my cane around the base to confirm that it was solid.

"Sideboard," I said. Of course I already knew that we had an antique sideboard in our family room. Even with my eyes closed, this wasn't exactly difficult. I continued up the hall past my parents' room, my room, the bathroom. I kept trying to move my cane back and forth opposite my steps, which is harder than you might think.

"Okay, let me catch up," Cam said. "Oh, sorry, whoops."

I opened my eyes and saw that Cam had run into the little table where Mom always kept flowers. He got out his phone and took a picture.

"Is that so you'll know where it is next time?"

Cam laughed. "It was my friend's idea. Whenever anything catches my attention — or if I bump into something — I photograph it."

"Why?"

"It's an art project!"

"Crazy kids," I said in a voice like some cranky old man.

"Crazy artists," Cam corrected.

Once we had passed through the kitchen, we were back in the family room, so that was pretty much it for our apartment. It was just the main floor of an old house. I sat down on the couch again, feeling surprisingly wiped.

"So here's the plan: I'm going to come back tomorrow and we'll have an outdoor orientation session," Cam said. "In the meantime, I want you to listen. Familiarize yourself with the noises around you. See if you can figure out where things are based only on sound."

"Like I do when I'm playing goalball?" I asked.

"Exactly so."

"Okay, I will," I said. "Thanks! It was nice to meet you."

"Until later," Cam said in a deep voice, like he was Count Dracula or something. Then he was gone.

I leaned back and closed my eyes, listening. At first all I could hear was a general hum of random noise. But then I started to pick out sounds: the steady rumble of traffic over on Cornwall Avenue. The occasional whoosh of a car going past our house. My mom and Cam talking in the kitchen. Then, right by my ear, a tiny chime.

I put one hand on the coffee table and felt around, unwilling to open my eyes. Tissue box. Water glass. Cell phone. I picked it up, sliding my thumb down the screen. Then I held the phone close to my face, blinking.

It was a message from Coach. It said: "Congratulations, Micah! You made the Junior Team!!!"

8 TRICKSTER

I kept rereading Coach's text. I was jazzed that I'd made the team but I wasn't sure Mom and Dad would let me go to the Regional Tournament. I mean, I wasn't even supposed to be playing goalball. And the tournament was coming up mega-soon. So I didn't know what to tell them, which, I'll admit, was unusual for me.

But I always come up with something.

I'm not saying that every plan I've dreamed up in my life has been a *good idea*. I've pulled a few numbskull moves. Like the time I stuck my head between two slats in our backyard fence to see if it would fit — and it did! The only problem was I couldn't get it out again. (Something to do with my ears sticking out like two open car doors, which they don't any more.) To free me, Dad had to borrow a neighbour's saw. He pretty much wrecked the entire fence. The worst part was, because we rent, we lost our damage deposit when we moved. Dad doesn't usually get upset, but that day he used a few choice words.

Then there was the time I climbed a tree and Mom freaked out and called the fire department. *Super embarrassing.* And I don't even want to talk about that fateful pancake breakfast Mom spent all of Mother's Day cleaning up. Still, I'm able to talk my way out of things most of the time. I only occasionally have to fall back on, "But I'm blind!"

I thought for a while, then hit on a radical idea. Maybe, this time, I should just tell the truth. Just upfront say: "I made the team and this tournament is important to me." The only problem was, I couldn't visualize how the conversation would go after Dad said, "Well, maybe . . ." Especially if Mom chimed in with: "Absolutely not!"

At practice that day, I stuck with the warm-up-only routine, as promised, even though sitting out of the games just about killed me. I dutifully ran around the gym. Then I chucked the ball back and forth with whatever player had the misfortune to be partnered with me. Finally, I writhed around on the floor pretending to block imaginary goalballs coming at me from imaginary directions as Brandon yelled: "RIGHT! CENTRE! LEFT!"

After all that, I had to sit on the bench, which was uber-frustrating. Especially since Liam was right in there proving what a total hotshot he was. Meanwhile, I was stuck hanging around like some kind of ball boy.

That sounds really bad. Maybe forget I said that — although in some sports, it is actually a thing.

The next morning, Mom knocked on my door,

saying it was time to get up. I couldn't figure out why I had to wake up early on a day I was staying home from school. But, when I walked into the kitchen, I understood why.

Some guy was standing there talking to Dad. And he had a dog.

I felt this heat start in my chest and work its way out; it wasn't exactly a good feeling. To be honest, I was slightly pissed. Then the dog came bounding toward me like something out of a movie. You know, with the whole *jumping up and licking my face* routine.

"Well, you two are going to get along just fine!" The man chuckled. "Don't mind Loki. He just completed his training so he's still very high-spirited!"

Really? I thought. *This is how he behaves* after *finishing his training?*

"It's okay," I lied. "No problem." I gave the dog a reluctant little pat.

"This is my son, Micah," Dad said. "Micah, I'd like you to meet Mr. Henderson from B.C. and Alberta Guide Dog Services. And you've already met Loki."

"Nice to meet you," I said as I stared Loki down. I'd never seen a dog like him: silver gray with deep blue eyes and a broad, smiling face. Loki wagged his tail and plumped down in front of me.

I had to admit he was sort of cute.

"Is he, like, an albino?" I asked.

"He's a silver lab," Mr. Henderson said.

"Wow! He's beautiful."

"He sure is! Labrador retrievers make superb guide dogs, but we've never had a silver one before."

"Well, come into the family room, Micah!" Dad said. "We want to give you and Loki a chance to get to know each other."

Mr. Henderson called Loki, who ran into the other room with his tongue hanging out. I followed.

We all sat there; it was awkward. My mom was all, "Very nice to see you again," so I guessed that discussions had been taking place without me. Loki sat obediently at Mr. Henderson's feet.

"What grade are you in, Micah?"

"Grade 8," I said politely, thinking: *Like you don't already know.*

"Excellent! Well, children's guide dog training usually takes place over summer vacation. We'll likely schedule you for July or early August."

There was nothing I loved more than being referred to as a *child*. I nodded slowly. "So I have until July to make my decision?"

"Pardon me?"

"I mean," I said, "I guess I have to decide before July?"

"I'm afraid I don't follow," Mr. Henderson said. He looked at my mom.

"Please tell us more about the training," she said encouragingly.

"Sure. The training is generally four weeks long. It covers care of the animal — proper harnessing and so on — commands, of course, and common routes in your neighbourhood."

Not gonna lie: I felt railroaded by the whole thing. I just sat there while Mom and Dad made conversation.

Mr. Henderson tried to include me: "You don't talk much, do you, Micah?"

Dad guffawed. "Quiet? Our Micah? Honey, did you bring the wrong kid home from the hospital?"

"I don't think I'd do that twice," Mom said in a bewildered way.

I didn't feel like laughing. "I'm just tired," I said. "Sorry."

"No, that's fine! Maybe this wasn't the best day to do this." Mr. Henderson got up. "Anyway, it looks like you two hit it off . . ."

I shook Mr. Henderson's hand and patted Loki on the head. Or maybe it was the other way around. Anyway, they left and I stormed into my room.

I was surprised that neither of my parents came in to ask what was wrong. Did that mean they knew? Or did they think I was just being a moody teenager or something? Either way, I was super relieved when Cam showed up. I heard him talking to Mom and Dad for a bit, and then there was a gentle knock at the door of my room. I opened it, cane in hand.

"Let's get out of here," I said.

9 RAGE

When I reached the corner, I stopped and unfolded my cane. I tapped one foot impatiently, waiting for Cam. At last I saw a blurry outline racing toward me using, I noticed, exceptional two-point-touch technique.

"What was *that* all about?" Cam demanded.

"Arrrgh!" I yelled.

"Nice sound effect," he said.

"Pfft." I sneered. "Feh."

"Not too enlightening ... Can you be more specific?"

"They never listen! They just don't get me!"

"Do you give them a chance?" Cam asked. "Do you even talk to them?"

"There's no point! They just ... they always ... they ..."

"Dude. Use your words!"

I shook my head, trying not to laugh. Nobody had told me to use my words since Grade 2.

"Breathe," Cam advised.

"Okay," I said. I put my hands on my knees and

took a few deep breaths. Suddenly, I felt way tired. I more or less yelled: "Forget it. I'm just being an idiot."

"You don't strike me as an idiot," Cam said mildly.

"You don't know me very well," I said. I felt calmer, more like my normal self. "We're not all hotshot master's students."

"Look, what's this about?"

"Goalball," I said. "I just found out that I made the Junior Team, which is a pretty big deal, obviously. But I know Mom and Dad won't let me play in the Regional Tournament!"

"Why not? Aren't you better? What did the doctor say?"

"He said my eyes are the same as before, so I *guess* everything's fine."

"Then why wouldn't your parents let you go?"

I shrugged.

Cam waited a minute or two. Then he said: "I wish I could get the hang of body language. It's one of my life goals."

"*I don't know!*" I said crankily.

"So let's go around the block — perhaps while practising our mobility techniques? — and then you can ask them. Do you know about shorelining?"

"Yeah, I learned that before," I said. I tapped my cane on the ground to find the concrete sidewalk, then moved forward. I slid my cane along the sidewalk's edge, using it as a guide. I started to walk fast.

"That's good," Cam said. "Shorelining works well on side streets, where there are fewer pedestrians. You should always use two-point touch in busy areas, though."

"Duh," I said.

"Do you, by chance, recall our earlier conversation? About using words, and idiocy?"

"Uh-huh." I reached the corner and turned right.

Cam caught up. "Micah, you're being a bit rude."

I suddenly stopped.

Cam crashed into me, then took a minute to compose himself. "I take it back," he said. "More like really out-of-hand rude."

"I'll tell you what's rude," I said. "A guy comes home from the *hospital* — and there a nice little guide dog there. A dog that was basically sprung on him, and, like, there was no choice for him at all!"

"Did I do that?" Cam asked innocently. "Did I spring a guide dog on you and then completely forget? Wow. That worries me."

"Not *you*," I snarled.

"Then cut it out! If we're going to be spending time together over the few weeks, let's make it pleasant. And not totally disrespectful."

"Okay," I said, calming down. "Does that mean I can be *a little* disrespectful?"

"Fine, but you've exceeded your quota for today."

"I'm sorry," I said, and I meant it. I knew I had to

get a handle on the rage-monster thing. You know the one I mean: "*You won't like me when I'm angry!*"

Let's face it, I thought, n*obody likes me when I'm angry.*

"Just don't let it happen again." Cam had that tone back in his voice that said he wasn't completely serious, and that I was forgiven. He took out his phone and snapped my picture.

The white flare nearly finished me. I held up my hand uselessly, blinking. "Whoa! Thanks for the heads-up!"

"Oh, oops!" Cam said. "Was the flash on?"

"Kinda." I rolled my eyes. "So I guess this means I'm part of your art project?"

Cam smiled. "Well, you most definitely got my attention."

So we went around the block — slowly. I told Cam what I was observing and what I was doing. And which cane techniques you should use in each situation, et cetera. In other words, I tried to keep my head in the game and actually focus on what I was doing. *Not exactly normal for me.*

We stopped at the front gate. "Excellent work, Micah," Cam said. "How about, next time, we take a walk by the beach? How far is it from here, anyway?"

"Sure. It's only a few blocks away. Do you want to come in for a lemonade or something?"

"I'd love to. But I wasn't aware we'd time-travelled back to 1955."

"People still drink lemonade!" I said defensively.

Cam followed me up the front stairs. "If you don't mind me saying so, I don't get why you're so freaked out by the guide dog thing. Didn't you apply for it?"

"Yeah," I said. I didn't exactly want my parents to overhear. "Can we maybe talk about it later?"

"I understand."

"Will you join us for dinner, Cam?" Dad called from the kitchen.

"I have an evening class, I'm afraid. I appreciate the invitation, though."

"Another time, then."

I grabbed a couple of Snapples out of the fridge. "Here you go," I said, handing one to Cam.

"So how were things today?" Mom asked.

"Great," Cam answered. "Micah's quite proficient already. He just needs to tune up his skills a bit. Once he's ready, we'll do some testing. And then he'll be official."

There was silence for a second. I guess we were all wondering: *An official what?*

"By the way," Cam added, "Micah has something to tell you."

I couldn't believe he would put me on the spot like that. "Uh," I said.

"Go ahead," Cam said encouragingly. "It's good news."

I took a deep breath, then blurted: "I made the

Junior Team. The Regional Tournament is next month. I really want to go." I clenched my fists, waiting for my parents' response.

"That's great, honey!" Mom said.

I couldn't believe my ears.

"Where will it be held?" Dad asked.

"Um." It was not the reaction I had been expecting. Had they been replaced by Stepford Parents? "The Richmond Oval," I said. "At the courts they built for the Olympics."

"I'm so proud of you, Micah," Dad said. "Congratulations!"

I totally had to give my head a shake and learn to trust people more or something. I couldn't believe I'd gotten myself so worked up about nothing at all! I felt like a freak. A relieved, relatively *happy* freak, but still . . . I guess, like Coach always said, I needed to learn how to control my emotions. And maybe even relax once in a while.

Dad gave me a ride to goalball practice that night and talked practically the entire way. About how great it was that I made the team, and how well Cam thought I was doing. And how things were generally looking up.

I couldn't really argue with that.

10 LIAM

So, the no-play rule was lifted. Liam, Sebastian, and Brandon were going to be against Brad, Lauren, and me. *No problem,* I thought, *piece of cake.* Brad called Centre and Lauren, Left Wing. So I was the Right Winger — not exactly my strongest position.

I slid my eyeshades down and everything went black. I remembered how, when I first started playing goalball, I'd close my eyes tight. It was habit, I guess, or maybe just nerves. Then I found out that I could concentrate more and — weirdly — visualize things a lot better if I kept my eyes open.

I tried to picture the opposing team. I knew that Brandon was probably playing Right Wing, too, because that was always his first choice. I didn't know where Liam and Sebastian were, though. So I listened.

For some reason, I suddenly pictured the guy from that TV show *The Listener.* You probably know the one: that guy who has ESP or something? I'm not sure how, but he can hear people's thoughts? I remember

watching it sometimes before the Panicky Swoop occurred. But for some reason, when he's supposed to be
listening, they focus on his huge eyes, looking all far-
away and intense, which, I guess, is better than zooming
in on somebody's gigantic Dumbo ears . . .

Whump!

The ball had flown straight across the court — silent
until it belted me in the stomach with an impressive
sound. I had stopped it, which was great, but it totally
hurt.

"High ball! Liam, that's a penalty," Julie called.
"Micah, are you up to taking the shot?"

"Sure," I croaked, "I've got it." I scooped up the
ball and stood with it balanced on my hip, waiting for
the court to clear. *Was that Most-Valuable-Player style?* I
wondered, *or just Idiot-from-the-Valley style?* I found the
centre of our Team Area and waited.

"Play!" Julie called.

I ran forward and threw as hard as I could, spinning
the ball to the right side of the court. I wanted to get
it as far into the corner as possible without actually going out. The goalball rang each time it hit the ground. I
could tell it was moving fast.

It crashed into the opposing team's net.

"Point!"

Those were some very satisfying sounds.

"Way to go!" Lauren whooped as she returned to
the court.

"Yeah!" Brad joined in. "Maybe you need to get hit by a car more often."

"Ha ha ha," I said mirthlessly. "Anything for my devoted teammates."

This time, when Julie called "Play," I was ready. I was sure, now, that Liam was across from me. I slammed the ball in his direction every chance I got.

He blocked it every time, and I started to feel blood rush to my face. I wanted — no, I needed — to get another goal on Liam. I wanted to win.

Coach yelled, "Micah! Strategy!"

If we hadn't been in a practice, that might have been an Illegal Coaching penalty, because I knew exactly what he meant.

"Brad," I hissed.

"I'm here!"

I winged the ball in the direction of his voice. Heard it jangle as he hurled it across the floor.

"Point!"

Yes! I whispered exultantly. I decided to pass for the rest of the game: sometimes to Brad, and sometimes all the way over to Lauren. By the halftime break, we were up by three points.

"Great job, Micah," Brad said as we walked off the court. "Let me buy you a drink. Would you like warmish juice or warmish water?"

"Warmish water, please," I puffed. I was beat. What was I doing? Trying to prove myself? I guess, yeah. If

I'm totally honest: I was trying to show Coach I still deserved to be on the team even though Mr. MVP had arrived.

"Hey, Micah," Liam said quietly. "Sorry about that wild throw, man. You okay?"

"Don't worry about it," I said between gulps. "It was a workout for the abdominals."

"Well, I'm glad I didn't break anything!" Liam laughed.

"Try harder next time," I shot back.

And that was greeted by dead silence.

I finished my water and gave the cup back to Julie, who was also our equipment wrangler and hydration provider. "Thanks," I said coolly, and sat down on the bench. I wished somebody would say something.

"More juice, anyone?" Julie asked brightly.

"No, I'm good, thanks," Liam said, and moved away.

So I was sitting there alone. Again.

Nice work, Micah, I ranted to myself. Why did I always wreck everything? As soon as I started feeling positive — like maybe, you know, *I belonged* — I'd blow it. There was no doubt about it: I was socially awkward. But what was I supposed to do? I was trying to be a nice guy. Maybe I was missing some essential gene.

We kept the same teams for the second half except that I switched with Lauren and took over Left Wing. This was my position — the one I felt most confident playing. I was ready.

But the game seemed to take place without me. Brad, as Centre, blocked every ball. Then he alternated between throwing and passing to Lauren. It was effective, I'll admit — they scored another two points — but I was starting to wonder if I needed to be there.

Suddenly, a powerhouse throw came straight toward me, ringing loud. I threw myself across the wing line, extending my hands to the edge of the Team Area. The ball hit my legs and kept right on going. Or, should I say, it used me as a ramp and whipped into the net with a clash of bells.

"Point!"

Great. My only contribution to this half was getting scored on. And I was pretty sure I knew who'd made the throw. "Time," Julie called. "Good job tonight, guys!"

We weren't actually supposed to keep score during practice, although I always did. I felt a certain satisfaction that our team had won.

Coach called everybody together. "You all know that the Junior Men's Tournament is coming up, and then the Senior Championships will be in July. So we'll focus on the Regional Tournament first. The team has been selected. A few of you have been asking who will be starting and who will be alternates. The answer is: I haven't decided yet."

I heard a groan ripple through the group.

"We have time," Coach said. "I'll make my decision over the next few weeks and let you know."

"Thanks, Coach," Sebastian said.

"Yeah, thanks," I added, although I was starting to think I'd probably be an alternate. In fact, I was willing to bet on it.

Everyone got ready to leave, except me. I hung around, laughing at every joke and adding the odd comment. I wanted to talk to somebody who knew Liam. Why? I wasn't sure why. Maybe I was looking for his Achilles heel? I didn't exactly plan what I was going to say.

And maybe that's why it came out wrong.

I was fairly sure Sebastian and I were the last ones in the locker room. I scanned around, doing one final check as I slowly tied my shoes. I started putting away my gear. "So, Sebastian," I said casually. "How do you know Liam?"

"He transferred to Magee," Sebastian answered, "about, I guess, three weeks ago?"

"Oh, yeah?"

"We're in the same English section. I didn't recognize him, but then somebody went out of their way to introduce us. You know how it is: Two blind guys *have* to have tons in common."

"Naturally."

"Anyway, I remembered him from last year's Regional Tournament and brought him to goalball last week."

"*You* brought him?" I asked. I couldn't believe it. *Sebastian knew this guy was super good! So his first thought was to parade him over to be part of our team?* "You're not worried he's going to, like, bump you from the Junior Team?"

Sebastian laughed. "Should I be?"

"Well, I think that, you know, it's not fair when we've been practising this whole time. I think a guy should at least be here a year before he can be considered for a tournament-level team."

"Maybe," Sebastian said doubtfully. "But he's been practising in the Valley, so what does it matter?"

"It matters!" I said. I was basically making this stuff up as I went along. "So I'm going to talk to Coach. Will you back me up?"

"Wait. What?"

"Will you back me up when I tell Coach that Liam shouldn't be on our team until next year?"

"What are you even *talking* about?" Sebastian's voice was borderline angry. "I don't get what's up with you, Micah. You were never like this before. We used to be friends! But now you're all competitive and weird!"

"But Coach just said . . ."

"Coach just said the team was selected!" Sebastian interrupted. "He didn't tell us who's starting or anything!"

Now I felt ridiculous and my ears were getting hot. "Whatever. I'm going to text Coach. I don't want to be on a team with Liam."

"What's your deal?" Sebastian asked. "You don't even know him! Where do you get off being such a . . ."

Liam

I didn't let him finish. As I reconstruct the events — and I'm not proud to admit this — I threw the first punch. Sebastian put his arm around my neck, wrestler-style. He whammed me in the head a couple of times. I flailed back, getting him in the gut. We bounced down the lockers to the far wall, which I hit hard. I spun us around and shoved Sebastian, punching the whole time.

Sebastian pushed me away. "That's enough!" he said. "Do whatever you want, Micah." He picked up his gym bag and stomped out.

11 SCHOOLED

Eventually, I'm sorry to say, I had to go back to school.

If I haven't talked about it much it's because high school was hard for me. Elementary school was awesome because I went to this old, red brick school that only had about 200 students, tops. Plus, I didn't experience the Panicky Swoop that ended vision as I'd known it until the end of Grade 6. Most of the time, I was just a regular kid.

But high school? I'm not knocking Kitsilano Secondary. I have as much school spirit as anyone. I mumble the school song at assemblies and cheer the Blue Demons and all that. And a famous guy even graduated from there! You can see his grad picture in the hall along with everyone else's. I mean, *you* might be able to see it. I'm not so great with pictures. One blurry little portrait looks a lot like every other blurry portrait, basically.

It's just that now I was expected to keep track of assignments and study and everything — and I hadn't quite gotten the hang of it.

In class, of course, I used my magnifier — technically a 9X round stand magnifier. I kept it in my backpack at all times in case I ever needed to read anything. Which, believe it or not, did happen from time to time. For online stuff, I used my laptop and JAWS.

Go ahead: Make the joke. Everyone else does.

JAWS is Job Access With Speech — don't ask me how they dream up these acronyms. It's not the old shark movie that made everybody afraid to swim in the ocean.

I should have been able to keep up but I didn't. I always forgot my textbooks in my locker. I made messy notes and then never read them again. Practically every day there'd be some pop quiz or test I hadn't known about. My grades were, in parent language, "disappointing."

So it was no big surprise that, when I checked my daily journal, I found that a big water unit exam was coming up in Science class. Tomorrow.

I freaked, trying to remember everything I knew about the water cycle, salinity, drainage basins, glaciers, icecaps, ice fields. Which wasn't very much beyond the fact that they existed. Then I faced a hard truth: I was going to have to study. I brought *BC Science 8* home with me.

Cam and I were supposed to go to the beach but I felt nervous. Maybe it would be a good idea to do school work instead? Mom insisted on homework being done before dinner — normally not a problem since I rarely did any. I called Cam.

After a couple of seconds of static — I guess he wasn't sure he'd pressed Answer — Cam said, "Hello?"

"Hi, how are you? Uh, it's Micah." Small talk definitely wasn't my thing.

"Oh, hi, Micah. I'm fine, thanks for asking. How are you?"

"Not too good. I have a Science test tomorrow and need to study big time."

"Well, you did just miss a week of school. Can your mom write you a note?"

"No. She won't. It's a unit test we knew about from the first day."

"Oh," Cam said. "So, in that case, do you want to skip today?"

"That would be great!" I said, relieved. "Thanks for understanding."

"No worries! I'm working on a paper anyway and could use the extra time. So we'll meet at your place tomorrow at four?"

"Okay," I said. "See you tomorrow." I got off the bus and turned down my street. I unlocked the front door and hollered, "Mom? Dad? Anybody home?"

I was glad there was no answer. I went to my room, got out my textbook, and plopped it on my desk in a determined way. Then I found the water unit, got out my magnifier, and started to read.

"The hydrologic cycle . . ." also known as, the water cycle . . . I actually remembered most of that part. Woot.

"The cryosphere: frozen water on the planet," which sort of made us sound like the planet Krypton. Cool.

I flipped to the end of the unit. Only 48 pages to go.

"Crap," I moaned, resting my head on my desk. *Why hadn't I read this stuff when I was supposed to?* Mr. Chan had even given us a schedule. But of course I'd only followed it for the first two weeks.

I shook my head and focused. Near the end of the chapter was a large box of text I guessed was important.

"Karst," I read, "a landscape formed by the dissolving action of water on carbonate (dolomite, marble, or limestone) bedrock." I suddenly felt tired. I flipped back to the part about the cryosphere and read about global warming.

I checked my clock. I'd been studying for ages and nothing was sticking at all. *Hopeless,* I thought. I picked up my phone and dialed. "Cam?" I said when he answered. "I don't get it."

"Don't get what?" he asked mildly.

"Any of it!" I was starting to panic. "I'm going to flunk this test — and probably the whole course!"

"What type of test?"

"Science!"

"I know it's Science," Cam laughed. "I mean, are we talking about short answers, multiple-choice, or what?"

"Mostly multiple-choice," I said miserably, "which is bad because you have to pick the most-right answer out of a bunch of almost-right answers."

"I hate that," Cam said.

"Me too."

"Listen. I don't normally recommend this, but you have to cram."

"That's what I'm trying to do."

"Seriously, Micah, you don't have time to read it all. Here's what you do . . . Is there a glossary or definitions or anything?"

I moved my magnifier until I found lists of definitions running down the outside of each page. "Yeah," I said.

"Memorize them."

"All of them?"

"All of them. Word for word. If your exam is multiple-choice, those definitions will be on it. Even if they aren't, you'll learn a lot and can probably figure out any question on the test."

"Just the definitions."

"Read them, then look away and recite them back. Keep doing that until you know them."

"All of them?"

"Micah!"

"Okay, Cam. Thanks."

"You're welcome. Good luck!"

Before dinner and for a couple hours after, I

memorized definitions. It was frustrating at first. I couldn't remember much, in the beginning, but then things started to gel. I even started remembering things Mr. Chan had talked about and stuff we'd learned in films. And I could see how it all fit together, like how, when you look at a map of the world, you can visualize how all the continents used to fit like pieces of a puzzle.

Suddenly, I knew every definition word for word and felt like — for once in my life — I knew what I was doing.

And that was a good feeling.

12 WHEN PIGS FLY

I read through the whole test before I started, like you're supposed to, and I knew every answer.

Every. Single. One.

I had to slow myself down, to make sure I was filling in the correct ovals. Still, I didn't have to think about my answers very long so I finished fast. Mr. Chan seemed surprised. I'll be honest: I was surprised, too.

Since I was feeling unusually awesome, I decided to ask Estelle about her painting. So, as we got our paints ready, I said, to no one in particular, "What are you working on?"

"A study after Picasso, showing all perspectives at once," Estelle enthused.

"Pigs," Anna said.

"Uh . . . excuse me?"

"You know, Picasso?" Estelle continued. "How he painted faces from the front and the side at the same time?"

"I know what you mean," I said, and I did. I'm not sure Estelle believed me, though.

I turned to Anna. "And you're working on pigs?"

"Here," she said. "Have a look." Anna put her painting on the counter in front of me. "Where's that thing you use to read? You can put it on the picture, if you want. It's dry."

I took out my magnifier and set it carefully on the canvas. I took a look — at an extraordinarily pink pig with tiny pearlescent wings. I moved the magnifier so I could see its face. Its eyes were closed; its ears flapping in the breeze. It looked delighted.

"Happy pig," I said.

"That's what happens when they fly," Anna smiled.

"I always wondered."

"Now you know."

"Mine's a portrait of my sister," Estelle joined in, pointing to her easel.

I put on my science-nerd glasses. Thick black lines between each colour made Estelle's painting look like stained glass. It didn't resemble any Picasso I'd ever seen.

"Nice," I said. Then I thought: *Bonehead! Is that the best you can do? 'Nice'?*

"Thank you," Estelle replied, and went to work.

"I like it," I said. "A lot." I furiously slashed green paint onto my canvas.

"Mm-hmm. Your picture's nice, too."

That could have been better, I guess, but it wasn't

the worst attempt. The truth is I never knew what to talk about at school. Every guy was a rabid gamer. Conversations in the cafeteria or hallway all featured Xbox, PlayStation, Wii, DS — and don't even get me started on multi-player online games. Those seemed like a group project everybody was in on. Well, except me, of course.

I used to be quite good at Mario Kart, which is the closest I'll ever get to driving but, other than that, I was never into gaming. And that left me with exactly zilch in common with every other kid at my school. Honestly, I didn't have much in common with the guys at goalball, either. I just wanted to be good at something. I guess I thought if I told myself I was a goalball star, it would automatically come true. I believe in the power of positive thinking and all that — but there's actually no substitute for experience.

And everybody seemed to have more experience than me.

I planned to tell Cam about my Science test and the Close Encounter in Art class. But, as we started our beach walk, I didn't. Instead, words poured out. About Liam, and how I was probably going to spend the whole Regional Tournament on the bench. And how every other player was better than me. I ended up sputtering something like, "I'm not good at anything. I'm not even good at being blind!"

Cam laughed out loud.

"I'm serious!" I said crankily.

"I hardly know where to start," Cam mused. "However, I do hope you're using two-point touch because you're walking quite quickly."

"I am." I slowed down a bit.

"It sounds like you're going through a difficult time." Cam sounded sympathetic.

"Whatever. It's my own fault."

"How is it *your* fault?" he asked.

I hadn't told him about the whole Sebastian thing — the fight — and how I was probably going get kicked off the team now. "I don't know," I lied.

"It's okay to be sad," Cam said. "What you're going through would be tough for anyone."

"I guess, yeah, I'm sad," I admitted. "Mostly I feel alone."

"That's not a good feeling."

"Do *you* get lonely?" I asked. I really wanted to know. It seemed like Cam had experienced a lot of the same things I had.

"Sometimes, sure — but things got a lot better after I met my fiancée."

"You're *engaged*?"

"Don't sound so amazed! As I recall, I'm a reasonably good-looking guy!"

"Sorry," I said sheepishly. "Congratulations."

"Thank you." Cam grinned. "Listen, I know it's hard to meet people, especially in high school. What about your old friends? Did most kids from your Grade 7 class go to Kits?"

"Yeah, but we're all in different sections. I never see anybody."

"I never see anybody, either," Cam deadpanned. "Could you maybe make a plan to eat lunch together?"

"I guess," I said, although I would never in a million years beg somebody to have lunch with me. I had missed a lot of school during the Sad Downward Slide, and when I got back, everybody had moved on. My old best friend, Jim, had gotten a girlfriend — *Margo*, who had never liked me — so we'd stopped hanging out.

Cam and I arrived at Kitsilano Beach Park. I turned right, heading down the path that led to the seawall. "I guess shorelining would work best here?" I teased.

"Very funny," Cam said. "Actually, I want you to stop and listen for a minute. What sounds are particular to this place?"

I closed my eyes, which always helped me concentrate. "Seagulls right in front of me," I said. "And waves hitting the beach."

"You know where the ocean is, so you know where *you* are."

"Right, and judging from that lovely smell, we're near the garbage."

"Gross," Cam said. "Let's move on, shall we?"

I turned onto the seawall and, using two-point touch, headed toward the beach. The sounds of waves and shorebirds were on my right and, more faintly, in front of me. I could hear ocean waves splash against the rocks below.

Cam caught up with me. "Hey, Micah, I've been meaning to ask: Why does the idea of getting a guide dog make you so mad? They help in lots of ways, and you know they're total chick magnets."

"I don't want to be . . ." I searched for the right word. "Dependent."

"I understand," Cam said slowly, "but we all depend on each other all the time. We use things every day that we didn't make. We don't know how they work or how to fix them if they break. Even people who think they're *so independent* probably have to buy shoes."

"Where would we be without the shoemaker?" I asked.

"The tinker? The tailor?" Cam continued.

"Or the candlestick maker," I concluded.

"Well, no. Sadly, candlestick makers became obsolete after that whippersnapper Edison invented the light bulb. Although I understand that lights are useful to those unfortunates who can't find their way in the dark."

"The darkness-impaired," I said solemnly.

"Let's sit here for a minute," Cam suggested, tapping his cane on a bench.

"Sure." I plopped down and instantly folded my cane, the way Cam always did. "Seriously, I feel like my parents want me to have a babysitter so they won't have to worry anymore."

"Maybe," Cam said thoughtfully, "but 'babysitter' doesn't describe any guide dog I've ever known."

I sighed. "They could be right. I can't even cross the street without getting wiped out by a car."

"That wasn't your fault," Cam protested.

"Yeah," I agreed, "being visually impaired is dangerous!" I thought of goalball players wrapping their hands before games because they'd bashed their fingers on things. Then I thought about Sebastian. Finally, I said: "You know that stuff I told you before — about Liam and everything? I was in a fight."

"A full-on fight? Who started it?"

"Me," I said, "and now I kinda don't know what to do."

"You could try apologizing."

"What, like: Sorry I'm a jerk?"

"Something like that," Cam laughed. "Listen, the drugs they gave you at the hospital were basically steroids. Maybe that had something to do with it?"

"Or maybe I'm just a jerk."

"Talk to the guy. Explain that you've been going through a tough time and that you weren't exactly yourself."

"Okay," I said, but inside I was thinking: *I was myself, though. I'm sorry to say: I was.*

13 SICK CHICK

I didn't want to go to practice. I'd worked up a pretty convincing stomach ache. (Since I hadn't gotten around to apologizing to Sebastian yet, I wasn't 100 per cent faking.) But Dad was suddenly very pro goalball. Maybe he'd bragged about me to his employees or something? Now, out of the blue, he was all: "The tournament's coming up and you're on the Junior Team! You can't miss any practices!" *Rah rah rah.* So I had to go.

I changed and hit the gym, running fast to work off my 'roid rage.

Just kidding.

I held back and let Liam — Coach's new poster-boy — and Brad check the Team Areas of the gym. Then Coach put Amir and me on Brad's team against Marcus, Liam, and Sebastian.

I was rattled, I guess, because I couldn't seem to orient myself to the court. For one thing, Brad told me to play Right Wing, which always made every-thing feel backwards. For another, Sebastian was right there — and I didn't know if he'd said anything. Or what he'd said. I felt like Liam probably knew, and that he'd peg the goalball at my head this time. In other words, I had my guard up.

I basically never got it together the entire game. My shining moment was when I blocked a super-fast shot that knocked me out of position. I jumped for it and caught the goalball with both hands, sliding back toward the wall. Then I leapt up and threw as hard as I could, giving the ball some spin.

Meanwhile, had I checked my orientation? Nope.

So instead I hit the Centre. And by that I mean our Centre: Brad. I heard an "Oof" sound and ringing bells as he lost control of the ball. He chased it for a second, recovered it, and threw.

I'm sure we took too long and should have had a ten-second penalty but Julie let it go. We were either close, time-wise, or she felt sorry for me. My face was probably way red. I was glad nobody but Coach and Julie could see it.

"Sorry," I whispered.

"Don't worry about it," Brad answered, but he didn't sound happy.

I figured if I tried especially hard for the rest of the game, I could redeem myself, but no. On my next throw, I spun the ball diagonally across the court and straight out of bounds. *That's it,* I decided, *I'm passing from now on.*

A lot of shots came to me — for some reason, I was the King of Blocking that night. I'd grab the goalball and spin it silently to Amir, who was a genius at swerving shots into corners without ever going out. Or I'd zip it over to Brad, who could powerhouse the ball straight down the middle, scoring almost every time.

So it proved to be a good strategy.

"Great work!" Coach hollered at the end of the second half. "Let's all call it a night, okay? Everybody can go except Sebastian and Micah. I need to talk to you guys."

My heart lurched weirdly. I tottered over to a bench at the edge of the gym and sat down. I heard everybody walk out calling, "Thanks, Coach," and "Good night."

After they were gone, Coach said: "Were you two fighting after the last practice?"

"Um," I stalled.

"Let me put it a different way," Coach said. "The cleaning staff heard you fighting after our last practice. What was it about?"

"Well . . ." I mumbled. I looked at my shoes. I needed to tell the truth and deal with the consequences. "It was my fault, Coach."

"*What* was your fault? You're on thin ice, Micah. Talk to me."

I sighed and shifted on the bench. "It's just . . ."

"We both like the same girl," Sebastian blurted out. "Yeah. There's this totally sick girl? And we both like her."

I figured it would take a miracle for Coach to buy that.

"A sick girl?" he asked. "Sick how? Infectious disease?"

Sebastian laughed. "'Groovy' in your language, Gramps."

"Don't be smart," Coach snapped. "So what's happening with this sick girl now? Are we going to have more problems?"

"No," I said solemnly, shaking my head.

"It's all good," Sebastian agreed. "There's no competition, and Micah knows it. He completely backed off."

I bit my lip so I wouldn't laugh. "It's true," I said, "Sebastian's a sick chick magnet."

"Good," Coach concluded with a meaningful stare. "Don't let it happen again. Micah, you remember our talk about sportsmanship? You guys are on the same team. I want to see you supporting each other, on and off the court. Now you'd better go. Your folks are waiting." Sebastian and I shuffled to the locker room, looking all subdued.

"Thanks, man," I said quietly.

"Don't worry about it." Sebastian grabbed his stuff and headed out without changing. "I'll see you soon, Micah."

"See you," I called. I wanted to say a lot more but my nerves couldn't handle it. I was supposed to text

Dad for a ride, once practice was over. Instead, I told him that I'd take the SkyTrain. I needed time to think.

I walked to the station, fiddling with my phone. I had Sebastian's number because he'd texted me once to tell me that practice would start late. I'd saved the contact. I found it and hit Call.

I hadn't planned a speech, so I was relieved when it went to voicemail.

"Hey, Sebastian," I said, "it's Micah. Thank you again for covering for me tonight. You didn't have to — and I probably didn't deserve it — but, anyway, thanks, and I'm really sorry. Could you call me back? I'd like a chance to explain. Bye."

I slumped into a SkyTrain seat and folded my cane. Then I hit Redial. "It's me again," I told Sebastian's voicemail. "Remember how I asked you to call me? Forget it. I got nothin'. I just don't know what I'm doing, ever. That's the only explanation there is."

14 CEASEFIRE

In English we were reading *Holes* by Louis Sachar, which I'd already read a gazillion times because it's one of my all-time favourites. When Ms. Hays asked for comments, there was the usual dead silence in the classroom. Then I said: "The way all the plot strands come together is really cool. It's like, the whole time, everything happens exactly the way it's supposed to happen."

"But it's so fake," a guy's voice argued. "Like, how everything *magically* works out."

"Because it's magic realism," I argued back. "It's not true; it's sort of a fable. I think it's awesome how everything fits together like a puzzle."

"Excellent point, Micah," Ms. Hays said, ignoring the other guy. "And what is magic realism? It's when magical elements coexist with realistic details in a story . . ."

I was proud of myself. Maybe this could be the new me? Somebody who was motivated and paying attention and stuff?

I felt even better when Anna came over at lunch

and asked me to sit with her gang. Generally I ate in the library — where you *are* allowed to have food now, as long as it's not something vile smelling that will peel paint off the walls. Usually I hunched over my sandwich like a troll. As luck would have it, my mouth was full when she asked me. My answer was: "Mff? Just a sec ... yeah. Thanks!"

Sometimes it takes everything I've got just to be normal.

I jammed my sandwich into my backpack and followed Anna to the second landing on the west staircase. This was, apparently, their spot.

"Everybody," Anna announced, "this is Micah. Micah, everybody."

"Hi." I waved. I only hoped I didn't have mustard on my chin. "How're you all doing?"

"Good," Estelle answered. She elbowed the guy next to her.

"S'up," he said. "We're in English together. I liked what you said in class today."

"Thanks. It's the only book I've ever read, so I figured I should seize the moment."

That got a laugh. I guessed I was making an okay impression. My phone chimed so I hauled it out of my pocket and held it close to my eyes.

"Can I help?" Estelle asked.

"I'm good, thanks," I said. "When I need help, I'll ask. I'm not shy."

Everyone seemed extraordinarily quiet.

"I appreciate the offer! Don't get me wrong," I continued. "It's just that too much help is worse than no help, sometimes. You know what I mean?"

I guess they didn't because nobody said a word.

"Hey, I hope I didn't hurt your feelings. I'm glad you asked! Sometimes people just grab me and try to steer me around."

"People do that?" Estelle exclaimed. "Mega-inappropriate!"

"You're telling me!" I almost started boring them with Blind Stories but was saved by the bell.

As we walked downstairs, Anna said, "We have lunch here every day. You should sit with us."

"Thanks! That's nice of you, Anna. So, I guess, I'll see you tomorrow?"

"For sure!" Anna smiled and took off up the hall.

I looked at my phone again. There was a message from Sebastian: *Meet 3:30 modern burger. Come alone.*

"Weird," I said.

"You're weird!" some random guy yelled.

Dude, you have no idea.

So at 3:30 I went to Modern Burger, which was across Broadway from my school. I tried to join Sebastian in the first booth and almost stepped on a black lab. The dog looked up and wagged its tail exactly once. Then it plopped its chin back onto the floor.

"Meet Thor," Liam called from the booth's far

corner. "He doesn't have his hammer today but is still relatively godlike."

"Don't you mean doglike?" Sebastian smirked.

"Ha," Liam said.

I slid in beside Sebastian. "The dog I'm supposed to get is called Loki. Are they on an Avengers kick or something?"

"I think it's a Norse mythology kick."

"Makes sense," I nodded. "So, what's up?"

"I heard you're getting a dog, so I thought you and Liam should talk," Sebastian shrugged. "In case there's anything you want to know."

"How did you hear I'm getting a guide dog?"

"Coach mentioned it. Your folks probably told him."

"Seriously?" I asked uncertainly.

"Relax! People talk. It's not a state secret."

"It's just that I'm not sure yet."

"Oh, yeah?" Liam joined in. "Why's that?"

I sighed. I was here, and Liam and Sebastian seemed genuinely interested. I figured I might as well order food and talk to them.

"My *mom and dad* want the dog," I said. "They think I'll be safer or something. But I don't actually need one — at least, not yet."

"I was surprised when I heard, to be honest," Sebastian said. "It seems like you see okay."

"I'm lucky."

"Don't forget it's your decision," Liam said. "I really

like having Thor and, yeah, I do feel more confident. But he's a big responsibility."

"How come you never bring Thor to practice?"

"I do sometimes. I mostly get a ride so I figure he should have some time to hang out and do dog stuff."

"Like eat chips and watch TV?" I joked.

"Believe me, you don't want to know."

"What if Thor has to, you know, go to the bathroom when you're out somewhere?" I wondered.

"How about I tell you when we're not eating." Liam laughed and took a bite of his burger.

"Oh. Ha ha. Good plan."

I guess Sebastian and Liam had been spending a lot of time together because they talked like they'd known each other forever. I wanted to join in but it all seemed Magee Secondary–specific. Mainly about which teachers had been there probably since it opened (the school had just had its centennial). And which ones were actually zombies or other kinds of night stalkers. It was funny, but of course I couldn't relate.

"Whereabouts in the Valley are you from?" I interrupted.

"Chilliwack. It's the corn capital of the universe, you know!"

"That's why he's way corny." Sebastian laughed.

"Ugh!" I groaned. "Who's writing your material these days, Sebastian? You'd better fire him! But seriously, do you miss it, Liam?" Although we'd moved a lot, my parents and I had always lived in Kitsilano. I couldn't imagine suddenly being somewhere completely different.

"Oh, yeah! We lived right on Cultus so it was totally sick. We used to swim in the lake all the time. I miss that for sure."

"We should go to Kits Pool sometime," I suggested. "It's this huge saltwater pool that's right beside the ocean. It has a ginormous shallow area and tons of lanes."

"It's megamazing," Sebastian confirmed.

"Let's do it!" Liam grinned. "How about Saturday?"

"Perfect!" I guess I sounded overly enthusiastic because Thor's head shot up. He stared at me like I was the most incredible creature.

"I'm okay," I assured him.

"Is Thor gawking at you?" Liam asked. "I'm told he does that when he first wakes up. I wish he wouldn't, though. It's embarrassing having a rude dog."

"He's not being rude exactly," I said. "He just looks a little bewildered."

"Yup, this is who I rely on to get me through my day," Liam said teasingly as he patted the lab's head. "Thor the Bewildered Wonder-Dog."

I liked Liam and Thor. They seemed right. Later, as they merged into a crowd of people just getting off a bus, Thor didn't break stride. Liam was completely in control. They were working together.

"I get it," I said out loud.

"Good," Sebastian responded. "Is that what had you so stressed? The dog thing?"

"Kinda," I said. "It was everything, I guess. I'm seriously sorry."

"Apology accepted," Sebastian said. "I didn't tell Liam about any of this, by the way, and I'm not going to. So let's just put it in the past and forget it, okay?"

"Forget what?" I grinned.

Sebastian laughed. Then he held out his hand and I shook it. "Welcome to the team," he said.

15 NAVIGATION

The next time I saw Cam, we practised navigating intersections. Even though I joked about it, I was somewhat nervous. We walked across Cornwall Avenue — past the exact corner where I'd been hit — and up Burrard Street to Fourth. A bike lane ran beside Burrard. Then it crossed the sidewalk into Seaforth Peace Park. I had to (as they say) "use my available vision" while also listening for bikes. Mega-stressful.

"So maybe this wasn't the best route to choose," Cam commented. "We can go back a different way but this is still good experience."

"Yeah," I puffed. It was way noisy. Cars, commercial trucks, emergency vehicles with blaring sirens zipped past on my left. On my right I could hear splashing water — from the Flame of Peace Fountain — and the irritated-sounding honks of Canada geese.

Cam took out his phone and snapped a picture.

"Careful," I warned, "those freakin' geese are creeps."

"I'd hate to be goosed to death. Such an embarrassing way to go!"

"Your name would be in the papers for sure."

When we turned onto Fourth Avenue, the traffic was quieter but there were tons of pedestrians. The white cane was good for making sure nothing was in front of me, but I hated how people moved aside in this veering, exaggerated way. *We don't have infectious diseases, peeps,* I thought, *so relax!*

I must have sighed because Cam said: "Yeah, that's part of the reason I modified my cane. It's a tool. It doesn't define me."

I'll admit I hadn't noticed, until then, that Cam's cane was blue.

"Hey, I like that," I said.

"There used to be an eyeball painted on the end but that's probably worn off now."

"So it was a seeing eye cane?"

"Exactly!" Cam hit a mailbox, then stopped to take its picture.

"Fascinating," I stated in my best Spock voice.

"Hey, my show is coming up next month at Granville Island Gallery and you're invited."

"Wouldn't miss it."

"Great! Maybe bring your friends from goalball."

A few days before, I would have gone: *What friends?* But I actually had guys I could invite. I told Cam how I'd hung out with Sebastian and Liam, and that it had gone okay.

"So you're forgiven for your evil-doing?"

"Harsh," I joked, "but, yeah, we're good."

"Another example of Better Living through Communication."

We turned down Vine Street toward the ocean. It was so quiet I could make out seagull cries in the distance. I told Cam what I was hearing and how I could use those sounds for orientation. I know this probably seems basic. But, since my vision comes and goes, it's a good idea to know different ways to navigate. Try it sometime. Close your eyes and listen.

We were almost home when Dad caught up with us. "I'm glad I bumped into you guys! I'm planning to make my famous defrosted cabbage rolls and salad. Will you join us, Cam?"

"Thanks! That sounds great."

It was just the three of us because Mom was on evening shift. So while he chopped salad stuff, Dad asked Cam about himself. Cam told him more or less the same things he'd said to me.

"But what the *hey* are 'educational experiences'?" I asked. I was going for a fake French accent and ended up sounding amazingly like Coach.

"I try to find spaces outside the classroom where hands-on learning can take place," Cam explained, "like in parks and museums."

"You mean 'non-visual learning'?"

"Exactly! Putting kids in a tactile environment lets them experience the world in a different way. Plus, I like to encourage people to use their other senses, not just sight."

"I noticed that." I grinned.

During dinner, Dad asked Cam more questions about special education. I usually tuned out when my parents started fogey-speak, but this time, I was actually interested. It sounded like, the way Cam did it, teaching — and even learning — could be fun.

My phone blared the *Mission Impossible* theme, which meant that it was almost goalball time. "Sorry, Dad, but can I get a ride to the community centre?" I asked, turning off the alarm.

"No problem!" Dad winged the dishes into the sink. "Can we drop you somewhere, Cam?"

"Well, I'd like to go to Micah's practice, if that would be okay."

"Yeah," I said, "you should both come to goalball!"

"That would be great," Dad said in a baffled way. Maybe he'd never realized that he could watch goalball practice. Then again, I guess I'd never invited him.

Then — because I'm a pro at choosing the right moment — I announced: "I don't want a guide dog."

"Wait . . . Don't you think that's something we should discuss as a family, Micah?"

"I thought it was my choice," I protested.

"Yes and no. I'd just like your mom to be in on this."

"I don't need one right now. Maybe later — okay. But I still have a lot of vision, and I'm sure someone else needs Loki more."

"That may be true," Dad mused, "but you're at the top of the waiting list so it's your turn."

I didn't know how to explain it. I felt like a dog would stand between me and everybody else, which doesn't make sense, I know. It wasn't that way for Thor and Liam, but Liam was different. He was a lot better at making friends, for one thing. I felt like I was just getting started.

According to my dad, our family had always been three star trails tracking across the horizon in perfect alignment. But that was beginning to change. I decided to explain it in his language. "I'm in a good orbit now, okay? And a guide dog will be like an asteroid that knocks me into a different one."

Dad laughed. "Maybe the new orbit will be better."

"But maybe it won't! I like how things are going and I want to see where they'll take me."

After a nearly silent — only slightly uncomfortable — ride to Collins Community Centre, Dad stopped the car and looked at me. He looked right at me, like it was the first time he'd actually seen me in quite a while. Then he said: "If that's your decision, Micah, I'll respect it. We'll talk to Mom and then I'll call the people at B.C. and Alberta Guide Dog Services." He let Cam and me out of the car and went to find parking.

"You handled that well, Micah," Cam said. "I'm proud of you."

"Thanks." I felt a bit dizzy. It was weird not doing what my parents said. I knew they wanted the best for me, and meant well, but they didn't always know everything. Sometimes a person needs to follow his own trajectory.

Knowing that I had spectators made me nervous, but in a good way. I put a ton of energy into the floor exercises, where we practised blocking to the right, in the centre, then to the left about a million times. I was definitely warmed up by the time we started the game.

Coach put me with Sebastian and Liam against Brandon, Amir, and Brad.

"You like to be Left Wing, yeah?" Sebastian asked.

"Definitely."

"Perfect! I'll be Centre. Okay, Liam?"

"Got it," he said, taking Right Wing.

Brad, Amir, and Brandon were all on the Senior Team — and two of them were Paralympians — so I expected we'd get our butts kicked. But that's not what happened.

Sebastian was nearly as fast as Brad. Liam's throwing was almost as powerful as Brandon's. And me? Okay, I wasn't as good as Amir but I made a few decent shots. A lot of players gain speed with a 360 turn, but my orientation wasn't good enough yet. I'd check my direction, take three or four strides, and lean way over to bowl the goalball as hard as I could. A solid, straight throw that jangled the whole way was a beautiful thing.

That is, until the Senior Team caught it and fired it back.

In the second half, I blocked everything that came at me. When the ball bounced away, I'd scramble out of the Team Area, grab it, and pass to Sebastian. He'd slide it to Liam or sometimes take the shot himself.

Near the end of the game, Liam tossed me the ball. "Sebastian," I hissed, "where are you?"

Sebastian knocked on the floor, telling me he was crouched in the centre of our Team Area. I ran around him to throw from Liam's side, giving the ball a harsh spin that blew through the Seniors' defence.

And that shot won the game!

Okay, not quite. We still lost but not by very much. And, hey, we weren't supposed to keep score anyway so who cared? *Just wait until next time,* I thought, gritting my teeth. *Next time, it's going to be true.*

16 EYE CANDY

I wandered up to the west staircase landing, all casual-like. I figured that Estelle and Anna would be there. Also, of course, Estelle's Shadow. None of the guys ever used names so I still had no idea who they were.

"Hi," I said, checking to make sure I wasn't going to sit on anybody.

"Hey," Unknown Guy One said.

"S'up," drawled Unknown Guy Two.

"So," I ventured, "my friend Cam is having an art show next month. If anybody's interested."

"Cool," Anna said. "Where?"

"Granville Island Gallery."

"I love that place! Yeah, we'll be there for sure, right, Estelle?"

Estelle made an affirmative noise. Apparently she was busy smoochin' the Shadow Guy. I felt instantly depressed.

Not to mention stupid.

"Don't mind them." Anna smirked. "They're still at

the stage where they're joined at the lip." She writhed away from Estelle, who swatted her. "They've forgotten that they're separate entities," Anna continued soberly. "It's very sad."

I gave a fake laugh but actually felt so crappy I could hardly choke down my sandwich. It was, to tell you the truth, dry. I found my water bottle and took a slug. *What am I doing here?* I thought with rising panic. *What a waste of time.*

"You play goalball, right?" asked one of the Unknowns. "I'm Brian, by the way."

"Brian, hey. Yeah, our Regional Tournament is coming up this weekend. I'm actually going there straight after school today."

"I saw it on the news. A thing about goalball, I mean, not about the tournament. It looked all right."

"It is," I said. "It used to be the only team sport for the blind but now there's hockey and even a kind of football."

"Excellent. Where's the tournament gonna be?"

"At the Richmond Olympic Oval."

"You mean you play goalball on skates?"

"Uh, no. We'll use one of the volleyball courts."

"Derp," Anna added.

At least Brian could laugh at himself. "Anyway, good luck with it, man."

"Thanks!" Chalk up another decent social interaction. It was getting to be a habit.

After school, Mom drove me to the Richmond Days Inn — with enough clothes to last a month, it seemed. She was definitely cool about everything. She didn't even mention any recent discussions! That was great because she had a habit of driving things into the ground. She did double-check that I had my cane, though, and made me promise to always use it. But I'll give her a free pass on that: Once a mom, always a mom.

I met up with Julie and Coach and the rest of the Junior Team. There was Sebastian, Liam, and me, Marcus, Jorge, and Adon, a guy I didn't know. Adon was part of Coach's other practice group, and I guess Jorge must have switched because I hadn't seen him in forever. I wondered, more or less in passing, if it might have been a good idea to have us all practise together. But whatever.

We checked out the court, which was set up way professionally with brand-new nets and everything. We didn't play a game. We just did some warm-ups and a bunch of orientation drills, as I have already described in painful detail.

I was sharing a room with Liam and Thor, who greeted us like we'd been away for a thousand years. He must have been sleeping because he scrambled to his feet in a panic when we opened the door. If he could have, I'm sure he would have saluted. Maybe Thor was super excited to have his person back. Then again, maybe he just had to go. Just in case, Liam took him out for a walk.

After they got back, I discovered that Liam had brought his portable Wii and every possible version of Rock Band. Also, he had invited everybody over. He only had the guitar (which he hogged) and a mic, so the rest of us sang like some deviant, discordant choir.

You know how you think you've totally memorized a ton of songs? Once you play Rock Band, you find out quick that you only know the *choruses* and not a word of any of the verses. And you know those lyrics and notes that run along the top of the screen? Guess what? Useless when you can't see them. Once in a while, somebody would remember a phrase and actually sing lyrics, but mostly, we made up random sound effects and fake scat singing. We figured if we could get through a song without the game shutting us down as a total fail, it meant we'd won!

It was a crazy time, for sure. Coach brought in pizza for dinner, because what else would you have before a Regional Tournament? Everybody was talking at the same time and sort of shouting over each other. By the end of the night, I felt like we actually were all one team.

I didn't have the greatest sleep. But once that *Mission Impossible* theme began, I was instantly awake and full of way too much energy. I pulled on jeans and my team shirt, which was standard issue the evening before. I noticed that I was lucky number 7. It seemed like the day was off to a good start.

Liam harnessed Thor and I grabbed my cane. If our neighbours had planned to make a noise complaint about the night before, the spectacle of the three of us finding our way to the elevator would have shut them right up.

Hey, you have to take your advantages where you find them, you know what I mean?

During breakfast, the organizer welcomed us and explained that the tournament would be a round robin between us, the team from Vancouver Island, and the guys from the Valley. Each team would play both of the other teams. And the team with the highest score (counting both games) would win. Unless there was a tie. Then the tied teams would play another, tie-breaking, game.

I wish I could say we had a cool name like The Predators but we didn't. We were just Vancouver. I secretly nicknamed the other two teams The Big Islanders and The Valley Girls (even though they were all guys) but let's keep that to ourselves.

This was the plan: The Big Islanders against The Valley Girls and then us. After that, we would play The Valley Girls. Then the team with the highest total score would take home the gold.

After the organizer finished talking, the guys from the Valley all came over to say hi to Liam. If I were them, I'd be bummed that Liam was playing for an opposing team now. But they didn't seem to care. Liam introduced everybody — I'm not even going to try to tell you their names. Liam told them I was Vancouver's secret weapon and that they'd better watch out. It was a pretty decent thing to say, even if it wasn't close to being true.

We weren't playing first, but we still got into our gear and headed down to the court. After all, you've gotta keep tabs on the competition. I only hoped neither team would score a gazillion points and win the tournament in the first half.

And, luckily, they didn't. I watched closely. I mean, I couldn't see any details but I could tell how each team worked together. Stuff like whether the player who caught the ball would immediately throw it, or if they passed to each other, or what. Believe it or not, I got most of my information from listening.

The Island team's Centre hardly ever threw but alternated between passing to the Right Wing and Left Wing. The Valley team's Right Winger never passed. Every time he got control of the ball, he'd peg it straight ahead. An inkling of a strategy came into my mind.

The Big Islanders and The Valley Girls must have been evenly matched because they tied two-all.

"Listen up," Coach called during the break. "Liam, Sebastian, and Marcus will start. And the rest of you — be ready to sub in, eh?"

That's me, Micah Janzen: Secret Weapon; Bench Warmer.

I wasn't totally surprised. Coach had always dodged the question of who would start so I sort of figured. I took my place offside with Jorge and Adon.

"What positions do you guys play?" I whispered.

"Right Wing or Centre," Jorge answered.

"Same with me," Adon confirmed, "but Left Wing's okay, too. Which do you play?"

"Left Wing, but I can play Right Wing or Centre no problem." *Oops, did I say that?* I wondered. What I'd meant was: *I'm a good Left Winger and crap at everything else.* "Oh, yeah," I added, "I almost forgot the most important thing: Eye Candy." I made a gesture that included all three of us and was relieved to hear laughter.

So I sat out the first half and tried to focus. The Big Islanders stayed on the floor the whole time they weren't throwing. They hardly left their Team Area except to retrieve the odd wild bounce, which didn't happen very often. The Centre was still doing that pass to the left, pass to the right thing. It seemed to be working for them. And I could tell our guys were getting frustrated. Liam was throwing a lot but no shots got through. The Islanders seemed to have the goal completely sealed.

Then it was halftime — a whole three minutes — and Coach subbed Adon in as Right Wing. Liam let a few curse words fly as he slumped onto the bench.

"Language, Vancouver," the referee rapped out.

Then Coach told me to replace Marcus, who slapped my shoulder encouragingly as we passed.

I pulled on blackout eyeshades and the referee checked them. Then I crouched and felt for the wing line to make sure I was in position.

"Glad you're here, Adon," Sebastian whispered. "You too, Micah."

"All right!" I said. Mom and Dad were supposed to be here, and I didn't want them watching me sit the entire time. "I'm so ready!"

"Quiet, please," the ref said. "Play!"

The ball was in The Big Islanders' control and their throw came at me. I slid and stretched, stopped it with my feet. Then I jumped up, ran forward, and slammed the ball down. A bouncing shot slid smoothly between the Winger and the Centre. It landed in the net with an unfamiliar *whoosh*. I felt dizzy. After all, I'd scored the first goal of the game!

"Point," the ref called. "Play!"

Now they hammered me. The ball came in my direction every time — and fast. Obviously The Big Islanders didn't know I was the Blocking King. One time, the goalball landed squarely in my hands. Without even getting up, I passed to Sebastian.

He snagged the ball and, with a roundhouse turn, whammed a bouncing throw across the floor. It zoomed over the Right Winger's feet and — *blam!* — into the net.

"Point! Play!"

Sometimes a twelve-minute half seems to take for-ever, but not this time. We didn't get any more goals but we didn't let them score, either. Then the ref's whistle blew to announce that the game was over.

And that we'd won!

17 MVP

I guess I should specify that we'd won the *game*. As far as the tournament went, all three teams were tied with two points each. We went to lunch full of speedy energy, talking smack and acting tough. It was awesome to be in a place where you were *supposed* to be competitive.

After we ate, there was this waiting period before we were allowed to start again. (I guess, so we wouldn't get cramps and drown?) The next game would be us against The Valley Girls. After that, if any teams were still tied in points, they would play a final time. I doubted that would happen, though. I felt sorry for The Big Islanders. Unless a miracle occurred, they'd be leaving with the bronze.

This time, I was on the starting lineup with Adon and Jorge, who took control right away.

"Hey, Coach," Jorge said in a low voice, "I think Adon should be Centre this time, just to keep 'em guessing."

Coach nodded. "Good idea."

"I'm on it." Adon went to centre court and pulled on his eyeshades.

"How about I take Left Wing again?" I asked casually.

"Go for it," Jorge smiled.

I guess he'd figured me out. Still, I was good at being the Left Winger — not to mention Eye Candy!

I took my position in the Team Area and the ref checked my eyeshades. The Valley Girls' Right Winger — Mr. I-Don't-Know-How-to-Pass — was starting too. He was directly across from me. *Easy,* I thought. "Guys," I whispered, uber-quietly, "throw to the Right Wing."

Adon and Jorge made noises that sounded like agreement as I got on the floor. I knew that most of the shots would be coming straight at me.

"Quiet, please!" The ref called. "Play!"

We'd won the coin toss so we threw first. Adon blasted the ball across the court to the Right Winger, who whammed it back to me. I knew the guy could throw, so I angled my body forward to block the ball. I would have hated to form a sweet ramp for a fifty-kilometres-an-hour throw. Especially if it meant assisting a potentially tournament-winning goal!

And I didn't. I stopped the ball with my hands. Then I jumped up and returned the goalball to the Right Winger with a jangling clang of bells. He sent it straight back to me. I called to Adon and passed.

We kept up the pressure, hurling every ball at the Right Winger. I could hear his teammates talking to him. But I guess he was caught up in the moment or something because he totally took the bait. After his sixth throw in a row, the guy had to be getting tired. That's when I passed to Jorge, who roundhoused the ball at him yet again. This time, the goalball hit the net so hard, it hit the wall too.

"Yes!" I crowed.

Amazingly, we kept on playing. I mean, I was sure The Valley Girls' coach would ask for a time-out to substitute the Right Winger. But he didn't. And Adon immediately scored again.

At halftime, Liam and Sebastian switched in for Adon and Jorge. The Valley team had substituted their Right Winger — finally — so that was it for my strategy. Luckily, Sebastian had a few ideas of his own.

"Focus on their Centre," he whispered.

"You got it," I said. I wasn't sure why Coach left me in. Maybe because I hadn't been throwing much? Or maybe he wanted to see the three of us together? Either way, I was glad he did. A lot of throws still came to me. I guess The Valley Girls thought I was getting tired — and I was — but I upped my game and blocked like crazy.

I whipped the ball to Sebastian, who was playing Centre. I heard him call "Liam!" as if he were planning to pass again. But there was no time! Was Sebastian forgetting we only had ten seconds to get the ball back over the centre line? Or had he just gone crazy? Everything in me wanted to tell him how to make the play. I almost said something. But I held back.

I decided to respect his decision, which was sort of a big moment for me.

Sebastian didn't pass — he was faking us all out! A shot in the dark whooshed by the Centre's feet and smacked into the net, just like that. The sound of the ball spinning across the court and landing in that goal was a satisfying thing.

Then Coach called a time-out and subbed Marcus in for me. And did I hulkify, you may ask? No way. I was never so glad to leave a court in my life.

"Go get 'em," I puffed on my way to the bench.

"You know it!" Marcus replied.

I hate to tell you that he got scored on a few minutes later, ending our shutout. But it didn't matter. By then we'd won the game — and gold in the tournament — so it was all good! I'm reasonably sure everyone was happy not to have to play any more. I, for one, was definitely ready for a shower, real clothes, and food.

Mom and Dad stayed for dinner and it wasn't even mortifying. They were extra-charming and didn't tell any embarrassing stories about my illustrious career as a child. They were also a lot more knowledgeable about goalball than I thought. I guess I hadn't been talking to myself all that time. The planets must have been in alignment because, basically, everything felt right.

MVP

Getting the gold trophy most definitely felt right.

Hearing the Most Valuable Player announcement especially felt right because the MVP was someone who had shown exceptional strategy, sportsmanlike conduct, and skill.

I'm sure you won't be surprised when I tell whose name was called. Okay, okay, is the suspense killing you? The MVP, of course, was none other than Sebastian.

Who totally deserved it.

18 BLINDSIDED!

And me? After the tournament — thanks to a little thing I like to call the Internet — I became Most Valuable Crooner, or MVC. I started researching Rock Band songs and (what a concept) *learning the words*. I researched other things, too, for homework and that. But I don't want to bore you with my no longer disappointing — and sometimes even excellent — grades.

Sebastian and Liam and I just kept hanging out. Liam's family had this humongous big-screen TV, so as long as we went one at a time, we could even play Mario Kart. I didn't realize how much I'd missed zooming off the Rainbow Road and burning up in the atmosphere every ten seconds. Okay, so maybe there was no chance I'd ever win. So what? It was good for a few laughs.

Actually, a lot of laughs.

Sebastian and Liam even came with me to Cam's art show. We were walking down to Granville Island when a silver dog glided into my field of vision like a ghost.

"Loki!" I hollered like we were long-lost friends.

"Micah!" Lauren shouted back. "How do you know Loki? Are you the nutcase who turned him down?"

"I am that nutcase," I admitted. "It's sure great to see him! I know he's working right now, but can I pet him? Please?"

"For you I'll make an exception."

I was glad I had permission because Loki was already drooling into my hand.

"But seriously, Micah, thank you," Lauren said. "Cody was way overdue to retire so I'm thrilled to be working with this little guy, especially since I'm starting university in the fall. Cody can't handle those long days anymore."

"So what happened to Cody?" Sebastian asked.

"We kept him, of course!" Lauren said. "And we'll continue to spoil him rotten, full-time!"

"Oh, I thought you had to give guide dogs back."

"Some people do. I have no idea how they can part with their dogs, though," Lauren mused. "Anyway, I know a few that need homes. If you guys ever want to adopt a retired guide dog — not mine, of course — I'd be happy to help."

"Hey, I'd love to do that!" I said. "I'll talk to my parents and let you know!"

We wandered down to the gallery together. Cam was right at the front door, greeting everybody. I introduced Lauren and Loki, Sebastian, and Liam and Thor.

"Sick show, man!" Sebastian yelled over the crowd.

"I was going for 'gnarly' but I nonetheless accept the compliment," Cam shouted back. "Listen, I want to make sure you guys have what you need. The options are guided tour via iPod, volunteer reader, or independent viewing."

Lauren, Liam, and Sebastian all picked iPods.

"I'll go it alone," I said. The captions were blown up to probably 120-point type.

"Are you sure?" Cam asked. "I've got great people here."

"In that case: volunteer," I relented.

Anna appeared that very instant, all smiles. "Hi! It's me," she said.

"What are you doing here?" I exclaimed, because I'm just that charming. "I don't mean it's not great to see you! It's great to see you! I'm just, you know, kind of . . ."

Anna took pity on me and interrupted my babbling. "When you told us about the show, I called the gallery to find out the time and everything. Long story short, I ended up volunteering. So, shall we?" she asked, offering her elbow.

"Lead on." I followed her into the exhibit.

"Welcome to *Blindsided!* The photographs are arranged chronologically beginning in January," Anna explained. "First up, we have a surveyors' tripod lying on its side in the snow."

I laughed. "Cam never told me about that!"

"The caption reads: 'I unfortunately knocked over this tripod twice. Ever afterward, I'm told, the surveyors looked extremely nervous whenever they saw me coming.'"

"Brilliant," I commented.

"Hi," Estelle called, weaving through the crowd. "How are you guys?"

"Great!" I said. "How do you like the show?"

"'Hilarious' does not begin to describe this! Just wait until you see May."

"All in good time," Anna said firmly. "Now twinkle away, little Star!" Then she added in a fake airhead voice, "She's decided to call herself Star."

"Shut up!" Estelle whined.

"I'm making a rude gesture at her," Anna commented, "just so you know."

"Thanks for the visual."

We tracked through the months, looking at pictures of fire hydrants, trees, hedges, and gates. Sometimes there were street corners, all zigzag and out of focus. Then we got to a hall table with flowers, a furious-looking goose (have I mentioned that I don't like them very much?), a mailbox, and me.

I was sideways with one hand up, hair curling over my eyes, sort of smiling at the ground. It wasn't a halfway bad picture. Not bad at all.

"The caption reads . . ." Anna began.

"It's okay," I interrupted, "I'd kind of like to cycle back to this one."

"Well, it's the last picture so I guess this means we're done," Anna concluded.

"I hope we're not *done*," I said with unusual smoothness.

"Well, that depends on you," she said. "Do you have a phone?"

"Uh, yeah." I dug it out of my pocket.

Anna typed something super fast and handed my phone back. "There. Now you have my number, under 'A is for Awesome.' Maybe use it sometime?"

"Definitely," I said. "I will."

"Good." She smiled. "So I'll see you soon." With a wave, she was gone.

I shook my head, still grinning. I went back to the last picture, the one of me. I put on my glasses to read the caption: "I'm glad I bumped into Micah, a kid with a fantastic imagination and the driest humour imaginable — not to mention courage in tough times."

I read it again. I leaned against the wall and tipped my head back.

Then I thought: *I just remembered that today's my birthday.*

That's not the truth. It's a literary reference. To *The Great Gatsby*, if you haven't read it yet. And, for me, complete bull. Since I'm an only child, my birthday is generally celebrated from the beginning of June right through to the end. So it's pretty hard to forget. In a week, I would be fourteen. But I felt like, over the past few months, I'd grown a few years' worth.

I looked at all the photos again, lingering over the furious goose, the mailbox, and me. So what if I had to wear nerd glasses and put my face right next to the captions? What was wrong with getting close?

That's when it hit me, and I knew.

As long as I let myself get close enough, I could see everything just fine.

THE LOWDOWN
ON GOALBALL

Goalball is a Paralympic blind sport played by athletes who are visually impaired. The athletes wear blackout eyeshades so that all players have the same level of vision: none.

The game is played by two teams on an indoor court. At the competition level, each team has six players: a Centre, two Wingers, and three alternates.

The game is played with a goalball, which is about the size of a volleyball and is blue. The goalball has bells in it so that players can hear it and know its location.

Goalball is played on a rectangular court that is divided into two halves by a centre line. At each end of the court, there's a Team Area. Thin ropes are taped to the floor all around the Team Area so that players can feel where they are. There are also wing lines and a small centre line inside each Team Area to help the players orient themselves to their correct positions.

There is a goalball net behind each Team Area that

is defended by that team. Teams score by throwing or rolling the goalball into the other team's net.

Goalball is a fast-paced game! Once a team has control of the ball, that team only has ten seconds to get it back across the court's centre line. Players move — and often run — around in the Team Area to find the best place to throw. They signal to each other with sound (knocking, clapping, or calling) so that they know their other team members' positions.

Goalball throws are almost like super-fast bowling. The throw must bounce at least twice before it crosses the centre line.

There used to be a rule that a player couldn't throw more than twice in a row. That rule changed in 2014. Even though it's still mentioned on some websites, that rule is not included in the 2014–2017 International Blind Sports Federation rules.

Games have two twelve-minute halves with a three-minute halftime break. During competitive play, teams must switch ends at halftime.

It's very important that spectators be quiet during games because the athletes must be able to hear the ball and each other. Goalball players need to concentrate and react quickly while participating in this physically demanding, lightning-fast sport.

BE A PRO!
KNOW THE LINGO

B3: A *Paralympic* blind sport classification that means the athlete (although legally blind) still has some vision.

Block: A player stops the *goalball* from entering the net by *blocking* it with his or her body.

Cataracts: The lenses of the eyes become cloudy from scar tissue or old age.

Centre: The player in the centre or middle of the *Team Area*.

CNIB (The Canadian National Institute for the Blind): An organization that researches the causes of blindness and supports *visually impaired* Canadians.

Goalball: A blue rubber ball that has noise bells inside it; it weighs 1.25 kilograms.

Goalball court: An indoor court that is 18 metres long by 9 metres wide.

Goalball net: A large net measuring 1.3 metres high by 9 metres wide.

Idiopathic: A sickness with no known cause.

International Blind Sports Federation (IBSA): *IBSA* is an international organization that sets the rules for blind sports, including goalball. *IBSA* organizes annual World Games and is also involved with the *Paralympics*.

Iris: The coloured part of an eye.

Iritis: Inflammation of the *iris*, which makes that part of the eye swell up. This is dangerous because the eye's pupil can be scarred shut.

I.V. (intravenous): Medication is put directly into a patient's vein by an *I.V.* or intravenous medication system.

Panuveitis: Inflammation of the whole eye, which makes it swell, become red, and hurt. It can also cause extra cells to build up inside the eye.

Paralympics: The Paralympic Games or *Paralympics* take

place every two years along with the Summer and Winter Olympic games.

Team Area: The 3 metre by 9 metre area located directly in front of a *goalball net*. The players on each team must stay within their *Team Area* as they throw and defend their goal.

Uveitis: A blinding eye disease that causes *iritis* and *panuveitis*.

Visually impaired: A person is *visually impaired* if they have lost part — or all — of their sense of sight.

Winger: The player on the left side of the *Team Area* is the *Left Winger*, and the player on the right side is the *Right Winger*.

Wing line: A touch–based marker within the *Team Area* made by taping rope to the floor. Each 1.5 metre *wing line* (one for the *Left Winger*, and one for the *Right Winger*) is located halfway between the *Team Area's* front line and the *goalball net*.

ACKNOWLEDGEMENTS

With deepest appreciation, I thank my advisor Carmen Papalia along with Mike Lonergan of BC Blind Sports, Robert Lebel, Cherie Lu, Ahmad Zeividavi, Brendan Gaulin, Deacon Jones, Angel Lu-Lebel, Doug Ripley, and all the goalball athletes who put up with me at practice!

For your support and encouragement — always — heartfelt thanks to Bonnelle Strickling, Talisa Corrêa, Frances Whyte, James Sebastian Moozhayil, Fr. John Whyte, Craig Whyte and family, Sean Miller, Logan Wiltse, Marlene Pauls, and all of my friends at Langara Library, especially those in Technical Services and on the Media Team.

Finally, a big thank you to the people who created the following resources, which greatly helped me to research and write this book:

BC Blind Sports: www.bcblindsports.bc.ca/ graphic/sports/goalball/

Canadian Blind Sports: canadianblindsports.ca.

Canadian Paralympic Committee: paralympic.ca/ goalball.

Darren Hamilton. Goalball: www.dhamilton.net/ goalball/HOW_TO_PLAY_GOALBALL/How_to_ Play_GOALBALL.htm.

International Blind Sport Federation: www.ibsa-sport.org/sports/goalball.

Ontario Blind Sports Association: blindsports. on.ca/sports/goal-ball.

GOALBALL COURT DIAGRAM

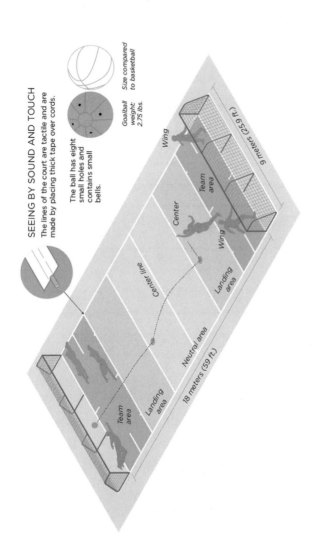

SEEING BY SOUND AND TOUCH
The lines of the court are tactile and are made by placing thick tape over cords.

The ball has eight small holes and contains small bells.

Goalball weight 2.75 lbs.

Size compared to basketball

Wing

Team area

Center

Wing

Landing area

Center line

Neutral area

Landing area

Team area

6 meters (25.9 ft.)

18 meters (59 ft.)

Courtesy of IBSA International Blind Sports Federation (www.ibsaport.org/sports/goalball).